The Pony Winter

Gill Morrell

The Pony Winter

Copyright: © 2007 Gill Morrell
Original title: The Pony Winter
Cover and inside illustrations: © Jennifer Bell
Cover layout: Stabenfeldt A/S

Typeset by Roberta L. Melzl
Editor: Bobbie Chase
Printed in Germany, 2007

ISBN: 1-933343-42-7

Stabenfeldt, Inc.
457 North Main Street
Danbury, CT 06811
www.pony.us

Chapter 1

It wasn't that I didn't want jodhpurs. Or the promise of a riding hat and boots. Of course I did. But you know how it is when parents give you something and think it's the best thing ever and actually it's just not quite right?

As I tore off the snowman wrapping paper, surrounded by my family – Dad and Mom and the eighteen-month-old twins, Holly and Tim – I felt the sort of warm glow of happiness that should always happen at Christmas. I squeaked with excitement as I unwrapped the soft beige material, with the special stitching and shaping which make jodhpurs perfectly comfortable to wear on horseback. After holey leggings and bulky sweatpants, they'd be fantastic.

"Look in the pocket, Jess," Dad urged.

There was a Christmas card with a picture of a robin and inside it Dad had written:

Dear Jess,
Have a wonderful Christmas
When the shops open, we promise you a pair of riding boots and a riding hat
Lots of love,
Mom and Dad

They'd even drawn a picture of me wearing all the right clothes and sitting on a gray pony.

I jumped up and hugged them both and then hugged the twins who'd started yelling at all the excitement.

"Thank you – it's a great present," I said happily. "And even better that I can choose the boots and hat myself!"

"There's more," said Mom, smiling in a teasing sort of way.

I guessed what was coming. A promise for me to go back to the farm where I'd been twice already, where I'd learned to ride, first on Tim (the gray pony in the drawing) and then on Bilbo. A chance to meet new horse-crazy friends and catch up with the old ones. A promise to spend another blissful week riding, cantering and jumping in beautiful wild countryside. My insides curled up into a knot of happiness at the thought.

"We'll pay for you to have six lessons at the riding school!"

I could tell Dad knew he was giving me a perfect present.

My mouth dropped open but I couldn't think of anything to say. A year ago, I'd have been thrilled to have the chance to have lessons. But last summer, I'd been allowed one lesson at the only local riding school as a special treat and I'd hated it – not that I'd told Mom or Dad. The instructor had been mean, the pony had been too strong for me, the other riders had ignored me except when they snickered at me for making mistakes, and then I'd fallen off and been winded. It nearly made me give up riding for life, but luckily soon after my friend Rosie from the first pony vacation invited me to take her sister's place on a horse camping trip, and after that I loved riding more than ever. Even though I fell off lots of times.

"Just look at her," teased Dad. "So amazed she can't even close her mouth! It's all true, Jess."

"We could see how much you love riding when we watched you at the horse show last summer," added Mom, "and how good at it you're going to be."

"So we thought, if we give you this, then maybe you can get a Saturday job, now that you're 14, and earn enough for more lessons."

I couldn't tell them I wouldn't go back to that riding school in a million years. Instead, I forced a smile.

"It's a cool present," I lied. "The best ever. I'll go and try on the jodhpurs, okay?"

I shot upstairs away from everyone and shut myself into my room. The jodhpurs were beautiful, the hat and boots would be perfect; maybe I should try to enjoy the riding school? But inside I just knew that I wouldn't do well there. It wasn't my sort of place. Everyone there wore all the right clothes and knew each other since birth and probably had gobs of money. And there wasn't anywhere else we could get to – we lived in the middle of a big town and there wasn't much space for riding.

I tried the jodhpurs on and they fitted with a little room to spare, so as to allow for me to grow, but they didn't make

me look fat; in fact, I thought I looked pretty good in them. I tied my hair – which I was growing longer – into a neat, dark braid and put on a V necked sweater and admired my reflection. I looked at the Christmas card I'd gotten from Phil, who I sort of went out with the second time I was at the farm, and wondered whether he'd think I looked nice. By the time Mom called to say the food was ready, I was able to sound genuinely happy and grateful, and after that it was the usual Christmas mixture of too much to eat, family walks and sentimental old films on TV.

A few days later, Mom said, "You haven't asked about your riding lessons, Jess. Do you want to try and fit one in before you go back to school?"

I could feel myself going red – it's a real giveaway, but I can't control it. "It's a little cold," I said tentatively.

"Well, yes, but I knew that wouldn't stop you."

I remembered all the stories I'd told her about riding in pouring rain and still loving it. Then I thought of a better excuse.

"I ought to get the hat and boots first."

"Why don't we go shopping tomorrow, and afterwards I'll call and see if there's a lesson available?"

I nodded weakly. What could I say? Maybe the riding school would be OK after all. I was probably making a fuss about nothing. I remembered how terrified I'd been when I first arrived at the farm when I'd never ridden at all. Yet it had all been fine once I got started. Maybe this would be the same.

My best friend, Martha, came over that afternoon and said she'd like to come shopping with us, and her Mom even offered to look after the twins while we went – a truly noble offer, as they were at the worst age for mischief, big enough to get into everything and too little to understand why they shouldn't.

The three of us went to a sporting goods store that had riding clothes and we picked a helmet with a dark blue cover and some pony boots – not as long as riding boots or rubber boots,

8

but easier to pull on and lighter when it's hot, and cheaper too. We're not exactly poor but there's not much spare money around now that the twins mean Mom can't work. I used to hate them taking over our lives, but I love them now.

Mom bought me some beige string gloves, too, that wouldn't slip or get soggy like wool ones. I fingered the tweed jackets hanging in tempting rows but when I caught Mom looking I said, "Don't worry, I really don't need one of these. Not unless I start riding in competitions."

"Well, you did one last year," pointed out Martha. She'd never been riding but she liked the idea and seemed happy to listen whenever I wanted to tell her long, complicated pony stories.

"Yes, but it's OK when you're from a farm. Everyone knows we don't ride all the time so as long as we look tidy that's enough. Of course, Georgie and Camilla had all the right gear, but I think they looked stupid out trail riding in all that stuff."

Mom was looking at the back protectors now, and I explained that they'd be needed if I did a lot of serious riding, especially cross-country.

"But that's what you did all the time!" Mom said, alarmed. "You went out across country every day."

"That's not the same thing," I explained. "*Cross*-country competitions are when you ride a really difficult course over natural obstacles like logs and high walls. Not like trail riding."

"I never realized it was all so complicated," Mom said. "Are you sure you don't need anything else?"

Wow, I thought, this is a quick change of heart. She's always made me manage by borrowing and wearing rubber boots, before. But to be honest I knew it was just being in the shop that was getting to Mom, so I dragged her away. After she'd paid we went to have some lunch, and that's when she found out how I felt about the riding school.

"You could have mentioned all this before I bought everything," she said, obviously annoyed.

"It's not that I don't want to ride …"

"I get the feeling you only want to ride if it's on your particular terms, Jess," Mom cut in. "Well, I'm not sure that's acceptable. You're lucky enough to have this chance to do what you say you want more than anything else; take it."

I exchanged glances with Martha, hoping that she'd say something helpful. I'd purposely brought it all into the open in front of her so that Mom wouldn't be able to be too angry with me. But she just raised her shoulders and made a face in apparent despair and kept quiet.

Mom did feel inhibited, though, and didn't go on about it, and by the time we were back home there were the babies to deal with. I could feel her looking at me, every now and then, and I felt really bad. I did my best to be useful and took Tim off to play so she could spend quality time with Holly, which is one of the problems of having twins. She always had lots of time for me when I was little.

Before going to bed, I made up my mind to sort things out. I said I was sorry and that I could see I was being silly, and I said I'd willingly go to the riding school for lessons, but I asked if we could wait for a few weeks till the weather got better. And Mom and Dad both looked very pleased and hugged me and said how sensible I was being.

But it didn't make me feel any better.

Nothing exciting happened for the next couple of weeks. School started and it rained or sleeted almost every day, and it seemed impossible that only a few months ago I'd been riding Bilbo over heathery hillsides and through lakes and even up hidden mountain paths. I hung my riding hat where I could see it from my bed and I wore the jodhpurs and boots sometimes while I was doing my homework, just to pretend, and I tried not to think about looking stupid at the riding school and to remind myself that I could ride much better after the trail riding week, anyway.

Then, one day a letter was waiting for me when I came

home. It was from Mr. Butler, who ran the farm, and it was like a message from heaven. It solved all my problems.

There was going to be a special week at winter break, only a month away, concentrating on pony management. I wasn't sure what that meant, but I got the feeling it was a way of getting around the fact that in late February the weather might not allow much actual riding. The letter said there'd be sessions on pony care, riding lessons, trail riding, and indoor activities.

I didn't say anything to Mom about it. Instead, I phoned Rosie, who'd been my best friend on the first vacation, though we hadn't gotten along so well the second time, and asked if she was going.

"I'd love to," she said, "but we're going skiing, the whole family. Kate's decided it's her favorite sport and she's never even been yet. She keeps going on about ski instructors."

I laughed. Kate had gone *off* ponies after she broke her arm, but also she'd gotten really into boys and looking good.

"She won't look so great when she falls over," Rosie went on. "We've been practicing at a dry ski slope and I tell you, Jess, there are muscles you use when you're skiing that I've never discovered before."

"Worse than when you start riding?" I asked, remembering how I could hardly move on the second day.

"Far worse. Still, it should be a lot of fun. It's a pity about the riding. I'd have liked to do it, but Mom and Dad would probably say I couldn't go later in the year if I went now."

I told her about my Christmas present and she said, "Well, if I were you I'd go for it, and then maybe try to get some money together by working, to pay for another vacation in the summer. It should get your parents off your back for now."

I wasn't sure I felt the same way about my parents, but then she came from a family where there was plenty of money for extras. I had mixed feelings about her not being there. We'd been so close at the beginning, and then things had deteriorated so much the second week.

Anyway, that left me free to speak to my other, newer, riding friend, Megan, who already knew about the Christmas present dilemma.

"I've been trying to get through," she squealed. "Mom says I can go in February if I want – how about you?"

I explained the situation and we talked about how great it would be, and I said I'd get back to her once I'd talked to Mom and Dad. Meanwhile, a text message had come through from Phil, who'd been on both vacations with me. It said, *"You're not going, are you? I can't. Please say you can't either. Phil xxx"*

I couldn't make up my mind about that. Was it sweet that he didn't want me to go without him or was it mean? It wasn't as if we'd been that close, and we didn't live near enough to each other to meet up; our "relationship" – what there was of it – had consisted of a little hand-holding, the briefest of kisses and a few text messages. There were times I really liked him and times when he could be such a pain … I decided to ignore his text for the moment and see what happened. If Mom and Dad said no, there'd be no point getting confused about seeing Phil or not.

So I went downstairs and over dinner I showed them the letter and waited for their reaction. I concentrated on helping Tim with his mashed-up spaghetti and didn't look up.

"I suppose you're thinking this could be instead of the lessons?" said Dad. He didn't sound too enthusiastic.

"If that was OK."

"I can see some problems. For a start, if you're serious about riding, you need some proper training, not just going out in a group all the time."

That's typical of Dad – he's a great believer in proper training. I squished some spaghetti into Tim's mouth and put down the spoon. I needed to concentrate.

"I know I always talk a lot about the rides, but we do lots of schooling as well. Hours and hours of walking around in circles being yelled at for not sitting up straight."

"That doesn't sound much like fun to me," commented Mom, rescuing the spoon just as Tim was about to throw it onto the floor. "Tim, don't! Eat nicely now."

"And they really know what they're talking about?"

"Yes. Mr. Butler's a great rider. He's got this amazing horse named Captain ..."

"Don't start! Does he know how to teach?"

We were interrupted again as Holly spat a mouthful all over her plate. I got a cloth and mopped her up.

"Sorry, what did you say?"

"Is he a real teacher?"

"Well, I'm not sure if he's got any qualifications, but the farm's got to be registered as a riding center, so he must have been checked or something." I was groping into the dark here. I had no real idea about any of this, but I was ready to say anything to persuade Dad. And Dave Butler truly was a great teacher, and he had Caroline, who knew her stuff too, helping him.

"I don't think we need to worry too much about all that," said Mom, to my relief. "All that matters is that Jess enjoys her riding and makes some progress."

"She shouldn't get into bad habits, though," reiterated Dad.

"I'm sure she won't. There are some very good riders who use the center, aren't there, Jess? Let's get the twins into their playpen and then we can concentrate, OK?"

Great – Mom was going to back me up.

Dad's next objection had to do with the weather. "It can be very severe up in the hills in February. Not like here in town. You might get deep snow."

I couldn't stop myself from grinning. "That'd be magical! We don't have to ride all the time, Dad. Just being there in the country would be so much fun. And we'd learn useful stuff about looking after ponies. Pony management, they call it. It's a real subject, like at school, with lots of theory."

I knew Dad would like that. He's always interested in exams and stuff.

"You really want to do this, don't you?" Dad said.

I nodded. "Please, Dad," I said softly.

"I think Jess should go," said Mom, decisively, "and in some ways it's a lot easier, her going at winter break. You've got a lot more homework this year, haven't you? After-school lessons could be hard to fit in."

"I know it's a lot of money, but I don't mind trying to pay some of it back," I suggested. "I'll try and get a job, as you suggested at Christmas."

"Don't worry too much about that," said Dad, surprisingly. "Things are looking up at work, and I should be getting a promotion next month." He took a deep breath. "OK, you can go. Just don't moan if it's freezing cold and rains all the time."

"If that happens, there'll be snow, and I can't think of anything better!"

I called Megan right away and we spent a happy hour gossiping about the riding center, sharing memories and speculating about what this vacation would be like. I told her about Phil's text, and she teased me in a friendly sort of way.

"What about Rosie?" she asked, sounding less sure of herself.

It had been awkward and hurtful last year when Rosie decided to devote herself to another girl, especially as that girl, Emily, and I had disliked each other on sight. By the end of the week Emily had shown herself to be spiteful and mean, and Rosie had tried hard to make it up with me, but I'd never trust her completely again.

"She can't come. Skiing," I answered.

"Oh. That's a pity. My friend who came with me before can't make it either."

I said, "Never mind," but I wasn't sorry; I liked Megan a lot and I didn't really want to share her with another best friend.

I phoned Phil later, and he was OK about my going. I said

I'd tell him all about the course afterwards, and we made vague plans to go at the same time as each other later in the year, if I could persuade Dad.

All in all, I was very pleased with the way things were working out. On the trail ride, Megan and I had gotten along really well, and I was glad there wouldn't be a threesome this time. There's a lot of truth in that old saying; *two's company, three's a crowd.*

But a threesome's what I got. The next evening Martha rang. At school, I'd told her all about the vacation and she'd gone home and persuaded her parents to let her go too.

Chapter Two

"Tell me all the ponies' names again," said Martha, as the bus began the long climb up into the hills that surrounded the farm.

I listed them all for the third time. It was cool to finally have a friend from home so interested in riding, and I truly was looking forward to showing Martha everything and to spending a whole week with her. Although we were best friends, we'd never spent more than an occasional night together, because we live so close. And she seemed genuinely bewitched with the idea of the ponies, convinced she'd love them all, even though I'd warned her that they all have different personalities and could even be bad-tempered or difficult. In fact, she accused me of being mean about them.

On the other hand, I was screwed up with worries about whether she'd say the wrong things, or not understand the way ponies are and how much hard work's involved in looking after them, or not like the farm and Mr. and Mrs. Butler who ran it, or the other riders. Especially Megan.

I'd text messaged Megan about Martha coming, which was a cop-out because I felt so embarrassed, and she'd texted back in a neutral sort of way. I just hoped she and Martha would get along.

Not that we'd be alone, of course. The first time I'd visited the farm, nearly a year ago, there had been eleven others including Rosie and her sister Kate, Phil, and a boy named Mike who'd been kind of hard work as far as I was concerned. Rosie and Phil had been on the trip in August with me, but that had been a smaller group. That's when I'd met Megan, of course, and a mega-good-looking boy named Tom, and the swanky twins – Camilla and Georgie – and the infamous Emily. I knew Rosie, Kate and Phil wouldn't be there this time, and Megan had spoken to the twins, who were – predictably – also going skiing. I hoped very much that Emily wouldn't be there, either, but I comforted myself that Rosie would've probably known and warned me.

"And tell me again how you get on the pony." Martha's nervous voice broke into my thoughts. I knew how she felt. I'd been terrified before my first stay and, like me then, she'd never been on a horse in her life. Reading about it is all well and good, but the reality comes as a shock.

I squeezed her hand. "Don't think about it," I said reassuringly. "You'll be shown everything and you'll be fine."

"Maybe I'll be the only beginner," she obsessed.

"I was and it didn't matter. Mr. Butler and Caroline are as kind as can be. They'll help you, and you've got me, too."

"I know, but I still feel I should know more."

I sighed, but I did sympathize and I was just about to start a repeat description of mounting when I realized that the bus was stopping and there was Mr. Butler, big and cheerful, waiting for us.

"Good to see you again, Jess," he said. "You're a regular now."

That made me go red, but for the best reasons.

"And you must be Martha. Nice to meet you."

They shook hands and he showed us where to stow our bags in the back of the van, and then we squished together on the bench seat and drove off into the hills.

The farm was quite a long way from the bus stop and a lot higher. The weather had been mixed at Easter and fine in the summer, but now there were heavy, brooding clouds and puddles along the side of the roughly paved road.

"How are the ponies?" I asked eagerly.

"They're all fine. And we've got a couple of new ones, a mare named Snowdrop and a biggish cob named Blaze."

"Impressive name," I commented.

Mr. Butler chuckled. "There's nothing much impressive about old Blaze. He's a real workhorse. But I needed a reliable bigger pony. We're getting more and more riders your age, and some of them are pretty tall and heavy. There's only really Campbell and Rolo who're suitable, and Campbell's been lame for a while."

"Oh no, is it serious?"

Campbell had been used as the pack pony for the last trip. He was beautiful and patient, with a long mane and tail, but I'd never ridden him. He was too strong for me.

"I'm afraid it's chronic laminitis so he might not recover. The vet's treating him at the moment, so we won't give up on him just yet."

"Poor Campbell. Can we see him?"

"Oh yes, he's not infectious or anything, though we have brought him indoors. He enjoys company and we haven't had any visitors for a few weeks, so he'll be glad to see you."

I made up my mind to visit him at least twice every day, and to give him carrots and sugar as long as they didn't harm him.

"You'll like Snowdrop," Mr. Butler went on. "But she can't be ridden yet, either."

"Why not?"

"She's carrying a foal. Due next month, we think."

"A foal! It'll be so sweet. Are you sure it won't be born this week? I'd love to see a foal."

"I don't think she's likely to give birth just to please you, Jess," said Mr. Butler, in the tone of voice he always used to show you were being silly. I went red again and stayed quiet for a while.

Martha hadn't said a word but as the van bumped over the cattle grid that separated the yard from the lane, she grabbed my arm and squeaked, "Is this it?"

"Yep, this is it," said Mr. Butler, parking next to the tack room. "Jess'll show you around, won't you? You're the first, I think – oh no, Megan got here earlier. You know each other, of course."

We clambered out and hefted our cases into the big stone farmhouse. It felt warm and cozy after the cold wind that was swirling around the yard. I pointed to the common room, where a log fire was burning in the massive fireplace. The room was filled with old sofas, a TV, board games and pony books, and the walls and shelves held horsy ornaments and horseshoes and pictures of the countryside. It was my favorite room in the entire world.

Martha peeped in and said, "Oh."

A bit more enthusiasm would've been welcome, I thought, but then I realized she was too wound up to speak normally.

Mrs. Butler came out of the kitchen, where she spent most of the day cooking us fantastic food, and greeted us warmly. Martha looked happier, and looked even more pleased when Mrs. Butler told us to take our bags to the triple room upstairs.

"You're in with Megan, of course," she said.

"How do you ever remember who knows who?" I asked.

Mrs. Butler laughed. "Well, I do actually remember most of you, especially if you come more than once, but I have a secret weapon, too."

"What's that?"

"My computer. I keep a record of everyone who comes. Up you go now, and then why don't you go and look for Megan? She's outside somewhere helping Caroline."

"OK. How many others are coming?"

"Seven. Five girls and a couple of boys. Go on now – I've got the supper to cook. Come and find me if you get hungry."

"Thanks," we said together, and we went up to the room I'd had twice now, although last time I'd swapped with Emily part way through. There were three single beds, and Megan's case was lying half-unpacked on the one nearest the window.

"Which one do you want?" I asked Martha.

"You'd better go in the middle," she said.

I'd have preferred to be in the furthest one, right up against the radiator, but I could see Martha's logic. We dumped the bags and then went to explore.

The wind whistled around the yard and I was glad I'd taken Mom's advice and brought an extra thick sweater of hers. It was longer than mine, so I didn't get the usual draft around my tummy.

I showed Martha the tack room with its rows of saddles hung on long pegs, and above each one bridle and bit set. She looked very impressed.

"But how on earth do you put it on the pony?" she asked, fingering the braided reins that I recognized as Bilbo's.

"Don't worry, it's easier than it looks," I said. "Look, this is the blanket I told you about that Bilbo has to wear under his saddle; it's got a special name that I can't remember. And here are the hard hats you can borrow. I always used this one."

Martha tried it on but it was too small for her. She has her hair done up in lots of little braids that take up a lot of space. We found another hat, one of the old-fashioned kind covered in black velvet with a peak at the front, which she liked better anyway. We'd had a happy shopping trip to buy her navy blue jodhpurs but her Mom said she'd have to wear rubber boots rather than leather boots. I'd said that the jodhpurs were the most important things after my uncomfortable experiences with thin leggings and too-hot sweat suit pants. She also had an ultra-thick padded coat, which I could see I was going to envy if it stayed this cold.

"What d'you think of it so far?" I asked, as we wandered down to the paddock fence with the great sweep of wind-blown grass beyond it dotted with gorgeous ponies.

"It's just as you said. Really beautiful. Mr. Butler's a little scary, though."

I laughed. "Less than he was. He's started calling me Jess instead of Jessica, too, so I must have done something right! Mrs. Butler's great, isn't she?"

We reached the fence. I automatically vaulted onto the top rail and sat with my legs dangling over. Martha stayed firmly on the yard side.

"Come on," I said impatiently. "They won't hurt you!"

"Are we allowed?" she asked nervously.

"Course! Look, climb over and we'll go and say hi to the ponies. I can see Tim … but where's Bilbo?"

I started across the rough pasture and Martha followed but kept well behind me. The ponies were gathered in a bunch at the far side, near the water trough and some bales of hay. When they looked up to see who was coming, several of them had hay trailing from either side of their mouths like mustaches. I made the special chirruping noise I always used for Tim and he lifted his head and looked at me with the most intelligent expression. I clicked again and he wandered over to me. I'm sure he remembered who I was; he should've, with all the attention and cuddles he'd had from me during both vacations.

I grabbed his head collar and pulled him toward Martha, who looked frightened but held her ground and didn't move a muscle.

"Tim, meet Martha," I said. "Martha, this is Tim."

"Hi, Tim," she said.

"Well, give him a pat," I said impatiently, running my hand through his silky mane and across the rougher gray hair on his withers, just in front of where the saddle goes. He snorted in pleasure and nuzzled his soft nose into the front of my sweater. The sharp smell of pony filled my nostrils and I leaned my head against his hard forehead and felt completely happy. Another whole week of ponies, and none of the troubles I'd had last time with Emily and Rosie. I decided then and there that even if Martha and Megan didn't hit it off, I wasn't going to let it spoil my vacation. The ponies were what mattered.

I looked around and saw that Martha had retreated a couple of steps but that the other ponies had noticed us and were standing together in a warm, hay-scented, shifting bunch, all those clever, kind eyes watching us and wondering if we'd brought food.

"Are you sure it's safe?" Martha checked yet again.

"Come here." I grabbed her hand and pulled her close to Tim. "Stroke his nose."

She put out tentative fingers and touched his velvety muzzle. He reacted automatically by pushing his head toward her for a bigger cuddle and she steadied herself and allowed her hand to follow the graceful line of his neck and down to his powerful flank.

"Nice?"

"Perfect. Better than I ever imagined."

"Well, Tim is just about perfect," I admitted, laughing. "But Rosie would probably say the same thing about Twinkle if she was here, and Phil swears that Bramble is the world's best pony. And I have to say, I have a very soft spot for Bilbo – look, there he is, the nearly black one."

"The scrawny one?"

"He's not scrawny," I said indignantly. "He's just naturally skinny. Watch out around him, though. He tends to bite when he's bored."

"You showed me the bruises," remembered Martha, eyeing Bilbo with distrust.

"I probably exaggerated. I got all sorts of bruises from falling off and stuff, too, last time."

I let go of Tim's head collar and he stepped forward,

narrowly missing Martha's foot. She stiffened and moved closer to me for protection.

"Don't panic, it's actually hard to get stepped on. They know what they're doing. Why don't I introduce you to all the other ponies?"

We worked our way around the group – elegant, nervy Magpie, stolid hay-chewing Rolo, clumpy-footed shaggy-maned Mr. Man, and all the rest. Martha gradually got more confident and stroked most of them, though, maybe wisely, she steered clear of Bilbo. I gave him a good pat, but I didn't give him the sort of face-to-face hug I'd given Tim – not till we'd built up a relationship again.

"Which one do you think I'll be riding?" asked Martha.

"It's easier to say who you won't have. Not Magpie or Bilbo – they're not for complete beginners. Rolo's too big for you, and the new pony, Blaze, sounds as if he is too. I wonder where he is, by the way? Poppy might be a bit small. She's great, though – very fast. Twinkle would be all right, or Meg."

I showed her Meg, a pretty mare with neat features and delicate feet.

"I'd like her," said Martha. "I love her colors – sort of speckled brown, and that beautiful dark mane and tail."

"Roan," I corrected her. "Well, you never know. Last time I expected to ride Tim again and instead I got Bilbo, and we got along fine together. After a while."

"Ouch!" Martha shouted sharply, pulling her hand away from Bilbo, who'd somehow sneaked his way around behind us and must have decided that life was getting dull. Martha had been waving her hands around and the temptation must have been too much for him. I gave him a push and he cantered away through the jostling ponies, looking much too pleased with himself. Martha was clutching her hurt hand between her legs and making agonized faces.

"Let me look," I said sympathetically. "I'm so sorry about this, Martha. It really and truly doesn't happen often."

"They're dangerous!" she said, her voice trembling. The ponies had picked up on Bilbo's excitement and were cantering fast down to the bottom of the paddock.

"They're not, it's just a game," I reassured her.

"Some game," she grumbled, but she let me look at her hand. There wasn't a mark so it hadn't really been a nip, just playful, but I suppose I couldn't really expect Martha to understand that at the moment. I couldn't think what to say to make her feel better. If I made a fuss about her hand, that'd build up the injury into something really bad, which it certainly wasn't. If I ignored it, she'd probably think I was being mean. And whatever I did, she'd probably decide now that horses were dangerous creatures and want to go home.

The ponies wheeled at the bottom fence and started back toward us. You could hear them snorting as they ran. Martha tensed and grabbed my arm.

"It's OK," I said. "Just remember how gorgeous they were two minutes ago. They haven't changed."

She stood her ground bravely as three or four ponies swept past us. They were having a wonderful time, pounding along on the cold grass with no riders telling them what to do. They slowed down and halted in a group some way off, wild eyed, swishing their tails and tossing their manes, and looking absolutely beautiful.

The other ponies had scattered and were grazing, heads down as they concentrated on chomping plenty of grass.

"I'm cold," said Martha, suddenly. "Let's go in and get something to eat."

She'd put her hand into her pocket and obviously didn't want to discuss the nip any further. We jogged up to the fence, clambered back into the yard and were just about to go indoors when there was a clattering of hooves and a voice called, "Jess! You're here!"

I spun around and saw Megan, riding a chestnut brown pony with splashy white socks, and next to them, Caroline, Mr. Butler's assistant, not on her usual long-suffering Micky, but on a big grayish brown pony that I guessed at once must be Blaze.

"Great to see you!" I called, running over and grabbing Megan's pony's bridle to steady him – or her – while she slid off. We hugged each other and laughed as the pony stuck his/her nose in between us curiously.

"You'd better say hello to Arthur," Megan said, patting his neck. "You've never met him, have you?'

"That's right," said Caroline, dismounting and giving me a friendly hug. "We lent him to a family who moved into the area for a while last spring, and then he was worked hard all summer so he didn't go on the trip."

"Wow, what a great idea," I said. "Can anyone do that?"

"What, borrow a pony? I don't think it ever happened before but I don't see why not. You'd have to move here first, though, Jess. Didn't you tell me you live right in the middle of a town?"

"Too true. I have no chance getting a pony of my own," I said gloomily.

"Well, cheer up! You're here for a week and that's three visits in less than a year. That's pretty good going. Anyway, who's this?"

Caroline smiled cheerfully at Martha as I introduced them. Caroline was very chubby, extremely jolly and eternally optimistic, and somehow everyone around her always felt better.

"You'd better get used to this," she said, slipping the reins over Blaze's head and offering them to Martha. "Take Blaze's reins and you can help me untack him."

Martha hesitated, but before she knew it she was clutching a handful of damp leather reins and Blaze was nuzzling her shoulder and snorting happily.

"He won't bite, will he?" she asked, alarmed, twisting away and trying to hold him at arm's length. It didn't work – he automatically took a step to catch up to her.

"Old Blazey? He doesn't know the meaning of the word."

"Bilbo took a chomp on Martha," I said, feeling responsible. "Just now."

"Well, that's a baptism of fire," said Caroline, checking Martha's hand quickly. "Bad luck. Your very first meeting with ponies and you have to get nipped! It won't happen again, don't worry. If Bilbo did that too often, we wouldn't use him here, but that's the first time he's bitten anyone for months. In fact, I'm not sure you weren't his last victim, Jess."

"Lucky me!" I said.

Caroline showed Martha how to lead Blaze. She had to hold the reins close to his mouth with her right hand, and then

26

she trailed them across in front of her and held the other end in her left hand.

"Tell him to walk on," urged Caroline. Blaze stepped out at once; in fact, I think he was leading Martha rather than the other way around. But Martha looked thrilled and Caroline winked at us as she followed.

That left Megan and me alone. We'd gotten along beautifully in the summer and of course we'd talked and text messaged since, but I felt awkward now. Would she be as I remembered? I glanced at her shyly and found she was doing exactly the same thing. We both relaxed and giggled and suddenly everything was back to where it had been.

"How come you're riding Arthur?" I asked, as we untacked him and rubbed him down. "Won't you be having Star this time?"

Megan shrugged. "Who knows? I don't think Mr. Butler tells anyone till the last minute in case of problems. No, I got here really early and Caroline said she wanted to exercise Blaze and make sure he doesn't have any bad habits, and she thought I'd like to try Arthur. He's so easy to ride, but I think he's actually a little boring. He didn't show much enthusiasm for anything when we were out."

"Maybe he likes being in a big group best?" I suggested. I scratched Arthur between the ears and he blinked sleepily at me. His eyelashes were to die for.

"Maybe. I hope I don't get him, though. I love Star and this would be my fourth time on her."

"What's Blaze like?"

"Another plodder, I think. Mind you, any pony bearing Caroline's weight has to plod. She got even bigger since the summer!"

"Maybe it's all the extra layers she's wearing. I look enormous in this sweater, after all."

"You don't! Anyway, you'll need it. It's freezing out on the hills."

27

I carried the saddle and bridle back to the tack room while Megan turned Arthur out into the paddock. Martha was carefully leading Blaze there, too, and I saw the two girls talking to each other. I decided to hang around in the tack room for a while and let them get to know each other. A few minutes later, Megan stuck her head around the door.

"You OK, Jess? Martha and I are going in for dinner. Coming?"

I felt a bit jealous. I wanted my two friends to get along, but it looked as if I wasn't needed already. Then I remembered what I'd thought about earlier, and reminded myself of how many times I'd agonized over whether people were being friendly or hating me only to discover that they were perfectly relaxed about the whole issue, and told myself not to be silly.

The big common room was full when we got back in. Obviously everyone else had arrived while we were out. I looked around quickly. Four girls, looking a bit younger than we were, maybe twelve, talked as if they were already good friends. An older girl on her own had her head buried in a book. And in the corner, engrossed in a video game, were two boys I recognized instantly. The smaller one was Chris, from the first vacation, whom I'd defended when he was being bullied. And his friend, unmistakably, was Mike, the bully I'd defended him from.

Chapter Three

"OK, settle down, everyone, and listen up!"

It was after supper and we were squashed cozily onto sofas and floor cushions. The fire crackled as a great spurt of orangey-yellow flame shot from the logs. I snuggled between Martha and Megan and waited to hear what Mr. Butler had to say.

"Welcome back! It's good to see you all," he started. "Most of you have been here before and some of you know each other, but make sure you get to know everybody else and that no one's left out."

We looked around at each other, checking out strangers as we'd been doing all the way through supper. I'd already said hello to the four girls, and I'd been right – they were friends and younger than we were, twelve and thirteen. Their names were Ellie, Natalie, Sarah and another Ellie, and to be honest I couldn't remember which was which yet, but they looked nice, and they all seemed to know a lot about riding. The girl on her own was still alone, perched on a chair near the door and looking as if she'd like to disappear through it. Her hands were tightly clenched by her sides and she only glanced up briefly through her long blonde bangs before staring at her feet again. Megan had tried to be friendly at supper but had gotten nowhere.

Chris and Mike, on the other hand, were being loud and confident and fairly irritating. They'd said hi to me in a perfectly friendly way when they'd finally lifted their attention from their computer game, but they hadn't made any special effort, and I didn't get the feeling they knew anyone else. They obviously wanted to make a big impression and had made lots of silly jokes all the way through supper, and were now lounging on the hearthrug, making sure they were the center of attention. Megan and Martha had heard about them, of course, especially Martha, because after the first pony vacation, which is when I'd met Mike and Chris, I'd told her all about what had happened about a million times. I'd helped Chris after he'd been dared by Mike to ride Mr. Butler's gigantic horse, Captain, up and down a rocky hillside at full speed, and Mike had hated me and tried to make my life a misery for the next few days, even though he and Chris had made up. In the end, though, I'd gotten back at Mike by engineering a situation where he got stuck in a boggy river. After that we'd become friends, and by the end of the week I'd even had the feeling he wouldn't mind being more than that. But by then Phil had also been showing an interest and, flattered though I was, I didn't think I could deal with two of them. Since Phil had been at the farm for the trip last time, we'd gotten onto sort of boyfriend/girlfriend terms, and I'd almost forgotten about Mike.

"I thought Chris was small?" whispered Megan in my ear.

"He was. He's grown," I hissed back. It was true; from just about reaching my shoulder last time, Chris had grown as tall as I and was getting quite good looking, too.

I realized that Mr. Butler was glaring at us and we shut up and listened.

"As you know, we're calling this a pony management week because we can't expect to ride out every day as we do in the summer," he explained.

"We don't mind," said one of the four girls. "We've got all the cold weather gear."

30

"The ponies might," he countered, "though, to be honest, as they live outdoors all year round, they probably won't. But just wait till you've been riding in the teeth of a February gale for an hour, Natalie. I bet you'll be longing to get indoors into the warmth."

Natalie didn't look convinced. Mr. Butler ignored her and went on to explain that we'd ride every day unless it was actually freezing or pouring rain.

"But we'll do lots of other activities as well, and they'll be especially useful if you ever expect to get your own pony. Anyone in that situation?"

Natalie and one of her friends put up their hands and the rest of us looked at them enviously. How great to be learning about pony management knowing that you'd be putting it to practical use with your very own pony before long!

Then Mr. Butler told us all about Blaze, and about Snowdrop, the mare who was going to foal soon.

"She's not going to have her baby while we're here, is she?" asked Martha, hopefully.

"Her *foal*. As I said earlier, not till next month," he said, more patiently than when I'd asked. Maybe because Martha was a beginner, I thought. "You can go and say hello, but not too often or too many at a time. If I catch you all crowding in there and worrying her, she'll be out of bounds. Understood? The same applies to Campbell because he's in the same building."

We all nodded, and I thought it was all sounding a bit too much like school, though of course I could understand why Mr. Butler wanted us to be sensible. I was determined to get out there to meet Snowdrop as soon as I could, whatever he said, and I felt a little bad because I'd forgotten all about visiting Campbell.

Mr. Butler wouldn't tell us which pony we'd be having till the morning. Last time I'd been devastated not to have Tim, but this vacation I found myself happy to have whichever pony he chose for me. Tim or Bilbo would be excellent, of course, but I liked the idea of getting to know a different pony and learning its special quirks. It was great feeling confident enough that I could ride more or less whatever I was given, compared with the first trip, when I'd been terrified, and the second when I'd been aware of how little I still knew. It made me more sympathetic toward Martha, who must be feeling just as scared, and I told myself to be really tolerant of how she might be around the ponies over the next few days.

Mr. Butler passed around a basket for everybody's cell phone. The farm had a rule that no one could use a cell during their stay, which we all thought was pretty pathetic, but having said that, the reception *was* almost non-existent and it *did* mean you could bury yourself in the vacation and not get bothered by home and normal friends.

We watched some television and chatted after that, but everyone stuck to the people they'd met, and then it was time for bed. Megan and Martha were hitting it off really well, better than I'd expected, though I suppose there was a logic to the fact that a person I'd like in one part of my life wouldn't be unlike a person I'd like in another part. They even looked similar; both black, slim and pretty. Anyway, we gossiped lazily about all sorts of subjects as we lay under the heavy comforters and looked out through the curtainless windows at the starry night sky, and I felt uncomplicatedly happy about the days ahead.

We scrambled through breakfast next morning so we could get outside as quickly as possible. The weather was perfect – cold but not frosty, with the pale winter sun gleaming on the damp paddock rails as we leaned or sat on them and waited to know which of the ponies we'd each be looking after for the next six days. The ponies weren't so bothered. They were munching hay from bales that had been scattered around the field earlier or drinking from the water trough or just standing musing like ponies do. They can be so restful.

Megan admired my new jodhpurs, which were mega comfy and made me feel so much more like a proper rider. The riding boots were a tad loose, as we'd bought them a size too big to make them last, but that had made them easier to pull on, and they looked great. I hadn't put my hat on yet, but I admired its sleek satin cover as it hung from a fence post. It was good of Megan to remember how much I'd minded being the only one without jodhpurs last time, and I was especially pleased to have all the right stuff because everyone was really well decked out this time. In fact, Martha was the only one who didn't have her own hat and boots.

Mr. Butler and Caroline joined us and we all quieted down as Caroline read out the pony list.

"Youngest first," she said. "Ellie – hang on, what are we going to call you two? Is one of you Ellen?"

The two friends looked at each other. The smaller one, who Caroline had been speaking to, said, "No, we're both Ellie. And our last names start with the same letter, too."

"Maybe we can call you after your ponies," said Mr. Butler. "Let's see... You're having Poppy, so we can call you Ellie P."

"And the other Ellie's having Twinkle so she can be Ellie T."

Ellie T looked pleased. She was the most nervous of the four friends and hadn't ridden much – though a lot more than I had. Twinkle was a gentle, easy-going pony. They would even match each other – Ellie T's brown hair would be exactly the same shade as Twinkle's glossy chestnut coat.

"Natalie, you're on Mr. Man again, and Sarah's on Meg; that means you four all have the ponies you had last time, right?"

"I had Star, but I don't mind changing," said Sarah.

"Good, because I think Megan gets priority for Star. Your third time, isn't it?"

"Fourth. I'd change if you wanted me to," said Megan, "but I really love having her."

"No, you're all right. Now, let's see, Chris, you were on

33

Poppy last Easter but you've gotten about a foot taller. How about Rolo? I seem to remember you like big ponies." She was obviously remembering the Captain incident.

"Wicked," said Chris, grinning conspiratorially.

"Martha, you're a beginner, we'll try you on Bramble. And Jess, after all the trouble last time, you get Tim this week."

"Great. Thanks."

"Gemma, you're the other beginner. Arthur."

Gemma nodded and went bright red. I felt so sorry for her; she must be so shy and nervous. In comparison, Martha was a bit tense, but looked happy and excited.

Mike was allocated Blaze, but he asked if there was any reason why he couldn't have Bilbo, and as there wasn't, that was changed. I was pleased someone would be riding Bilbo. I didn't especially want to myself, but I was fond of him and this way I'd see him and even maybe get to ride him.

"In that case, why don't you ride Blaze this week, Caroline?" Mr. Butler suggested. "Then we can get to know him. I'm sure Micky would welcome a break."

We suppressed giggles as Mike, unseen by Mr. Butler or Caroline, mimed a relieved Micky.

"Are there any ponies we're not using?" asked Megan.

"Mmmm, Magpie and Campbell," said Caroline, checking her list. "Campbell's lame, as you all know, and Magpie's cast a shoe, so it's easier not to use her for a day or two... OK, everyone, go and catch your ponies."

Almost everyone leapt over the fence and made a beeline for their pony, but Martha and Gemma stayed where they were.

"Come on, Martha, let's find Bramble," offered Megan.

"I'll help you catch Arthur if you like," I suggested to Gemma, slightly annoyed that Megan had jumped in so fast to help my best friend. Gemma went red again but came with me down the field.

"Is this your first time here?" I asked. I knew it must be, but it seemed an easy way to start a conversation.

But all she did was nod, so that didn't get us far. Arthur was waiting for us. I had the impression he was ultimately sensible which would probably make him a good beginner's pony but not much fun. I showed Gemma how to lead him and noticed that Megan had grabbed Bramble's halter and that Martha was now leading him up the paddock.

That left Megan and me to catch Tim and Star. I held out my hand toward Tim and he snorted in a friendly way and walked steadily up to me – a perfectly behaved pony. Star was friskier, and Megan had to chase her down to the bottom fence before she was cornered, tossing her black head playfully, but she did allow Megan to get hold of her rope halter and to stroke the little white patch on her forehead which gave her her name.

Caroline and Mr. Butler helped Martha and Gemma tack up while the rest of us did our own ponies. I retrieved Tim's saddle and bridle from the tack room and got on with the job. It was wonderful to slip back into the routine of sliding the bit into his mouth and buckling on his bridle and heaving the saddle on and doing up the girth. Tim, gentle and willing as always, watched me with mild curiosity. The intoxicating smell of ponies and the texture of his smooth coat and long, silky mane filled my senses and made me feel incredibly happy. Mounting was easy; Tim was a couple of inches – half a hand in horse measurements – shorter than Bilbo, and anyway I was so used to mounting now that even after six months' break, it was entirely automatic to face away from Tim's head on his left side, put the toe of my left foot into the stirrup, gather up the reins in my left hand and put my right hand onto the saddle and spring up, swinging my right leg over Tim's back and settling myself gently onto the saddle. Then I wriggled around till I felt comfortable, feeling for the right-hand stirrup and fixing the reins so they were distributed evenly between my hands, and pulled back slightly as Tim decided the moment had come for a little wander. It was so different from how unstable it had seemed less than a year ago when all I knew about horses was what I'd read.

That reminded me of the time I'd fallen off because the girth holding the saddle in place had been too loose, and although that had been Mike's doing, I knew that sometimes ponies blow out their stomachs when the saddle's put on, so I lifted my right leg in front of the saddle and pulled the girth buckle. Sure enough, it easily tightened up a notch, and I ran my fingers between the girth and Tim's tummy to make sure it wasn't too tight now. I sat up again and felt the length of the stirrups; they were a little too short. I fiddled with the buckles, careful not to let the strap slip through and lose the whole stirrup leather, and adjusted them so that my feet were at the right angle. I leaned forward and pulled Tim's ears affectionately to tell him I'd finished getting him ready, and then I had time to look around at everyone else.

There was a general atmosphere of purposefulness. Some of the ponies were standing placidly, heads down; others were fidgeting and looking excited; and one or two were already being walked around the yard. Caroline was helping Gemma adjust Arthur's stirrups and showing her how to sit with a straight back right in the lowest part of the saddle. Mr. Butler was holding Bramble's halter and talking Martha through mounting. Bramble tossed her head and took a step toward Mr. Butler, so that her hindquarters were suddenly further away for Martha, who just managed to land onto the saddle, and then hung on as if she was on the top of an elephant rather than a pony.

"Settle down, now," Mr. Butler told Bramble, who fidgeted and moved sideways. Martha gave a gasp and grabbed the pommel at the front of the saddle with both hands, dropping the reins, which looped slackly almost to the ground.

"Pick up the reins," Mr. Butler told her at once. "It's fine to hang onto the saddle for the time being, till you feel comfortable, but you must keep hold of the reins. You can't hope to control Bramble otherwise."

Martha looked as if she wouldn't mind giving up all control of her pony for a chance to feel secure, but she gathered the long braided string reins together and Mr. Butler tied them so that they couldn't drop so far.

"That's better," he said. "Now, sit up straight and look forward between Bramble's ears while I adjust the stirrups."

Martha sat very stiffly upright, trying to ignore Mr. Butler as he shortened the leathers. I was surprised at how small she looked. I hadn't really thought about it before, but over the last few months I'd grown a lot and she hadn't. I glanced down and noticed how near the ground was to me now and felt how still and sensible Tim was being. Then I watched Bramble mouth at her bit and shake her head impatiently, and I had an idea.

I squeezed Tim's sides gently and he walked over obediently.

"Mr. Butler," I said.

He didn't look around. "Hang on a moment, Jess. This knothole hasn't been used too often; it's stiff."

"Would it be better if Martha and I swapped and she had Tim and I had Bramble?"

He straightened and looked at me.

"Well, yes, in the sense that Tim's a great beginner's pony and also quite a lot smaller. But last year you didn't get to ride him and we know how much you missed him."

"I enjoyed Bilbo, after a while."

"Yes, but Mike's on Bilbo ..."

"That's not what I mean. I liked trying a new pony. Phil rode Bramble when I was here last time, but I'd love to have a try on her. And actually, I think I might have outgrown Tim."

Mr. Butler looked at my long legs and laughed.

"Maybe you're right, though you're light enough. Well, it's a generous offer. What do you say, Martha?"

"I'd love to have Tim, if you really don't mind, Jess?"

"Then that's settled," I said, slipping my feet from the stirrups and sliding off. It wasn't very far to the ground; Tim really was getting too small for me. "Just don't mind if I give him a cuddle now and then!"

Ten minutes later we were all sorted out. Martha was looking a little less scared on Tim's wide, heavy back, and I was feeling Bramble's mouth through her reins. I'd unknotted them, letting the slack lie in a long loop to one side of the saddle but ready to use it if need be to allow her her head when we went fast. I could feel her bubbling over with energy and excitement and I knew I'd made the right decision, not just for my friend's sake, but also for my riding education – and for fun.

Chapter Four

The long line of riders and ponies walked with a nice clip clop noise out onto the lane. Caroline, with Martha just behind her, went first, and Mr. Butler brought up the rear with Gemma. I was between Mike and Natalie, which gave me a chance to talk properly to Mike for the first time.

"I rode Bilbo when I came for the trail riding trip," I told him.

He twisted in the saddle to look back at me, one hand planted for balance behind him on Bilbo's quarters.

"Did he bite you?"

"Several times." I made a face and we both laughed. "But once I got used to him, he's a great pony. We had some fantastic rides."

"Lucky you. So, what was the trip like?"

I kicked Bramble forward and launched into a description of the highlights of the trip, though I skipped the part about me being accused unfairly. Megan came up alongside to add information, too. The lane was very quiet and we'd have been sure to hear well beforehand if a car came along, but Mr. Butler's voice soared over the noise of clattering hoofs to order us back in line. Megan ended up between Mike and me, so we couldn't say any more, but I was glad we'd talked and that everything was going to be easy between us.

The lane led to a gateway into a grassy field and we all gathered just inside, the more experienced riders checking girths and the beginners sitting as still as they dared. It was much colder than I'd expected. The wind was whistling up the hill and penetrating any gaps it could. Mom's gift of riding gloves was coming in very useful, but to warm up properly we needed a good canter.

Mr. Butler obviously agreed, but there was the problem of Gemma and Martha who hadn't even trotted yet and looked, to be honest, as if it was going to take them all day to get used to being on a pony at all. He had a brief talk with Caroline and then spoke to us all.

"As it's so cold, we're going to divide into two groups. The better riders can go ahead with Caroline and do a good fast circuit. You'll be back at the farm for lunch. Then Martha and Gemma can stay with me and we'll do some basics and meet you later."

"I don't mind staying and helping you," said Megan unexpectedly. "It'll give me a chance to get used to riding again."

Martha looked really pleased.

I thought, she's *my* friend, so I shouldn't really abandon her. So I offered to stay, too, and we helped to steady Tim and Arthur as the others streamed away down the hill at a fast trot that quickly turned into a canter.

"Well done, you two," murmured Mr. Butler. "Now, girls, let's do some schooling."

We spent a good hour in the field going through the essentials of riding. First, Mr. Butler got us to walk the ponies around him in a big circle, while he made sure we were sitting properly with our legs at exactly the right angle. I'd done it all before, but Megan was right, it was useful. It's so easy to get into bad habits. I tend to slouch a bit, and Mr. Butler must have told me to sit straight at least six times, but whenever I remembered I knew I was more balanced and in better touch with my pony. It was nice to have time to get to know Bramble, too. Phil had always loved her and I'd petted her, of course, but the way the farm worked meant you always concentrated on your own pony. I'd always admired her looks, though – she was dark brown with a black mane and tail, and held her head high in an alert, intelligent way. Her stride was longer than Tim's but very smooth, and I could see why Phil enjoyed riding her.

Megan's main fault was that she let her lower legs slip back, instead of going straight down.

"Does it really matter?" she asked.

"Well, it's all to do with balance. Your legs act as springs, you see. Think about keeping your heels down. Then your legs can't go back."

"You're right," Megan said. "For some reason, that's easier for me to remember. Just shout "heels down" at me whenever I get it wrong, Jess," she called over to me.

Meanwhile, Gemma and Martha were getting surer of themselves, and Mr. Butler encouraged them to let go of the saddle and hold the reins carefully, a little to each side of their ponies' necks, letting their hands move with the ponies' rhythms. It sounds like such an easy thing to do, but I remembered how difficult it was the first day I'd ridden. We all rode with our stirrups crossed in front of us for a while, too. Mr. Butler made us stretch our legs down as long as we could. The sensation of the pony's body moving under my own became much clearer, almost as it might riding bareback. It made me think that that was something I must try this week.

We were going around like this when Mr. Butler suddenly called, "Trot on!" and the ponies responded instantly without any aids from us.

Megan and I were fine; we were used to trotting without stirrups, which can be painful but is actually quite easy as you just jog along with the pony. Martha, in front of me, noticeably stiffened up and rolled around on Tim, but his trot

41

was very smooth and she stayed in the saddle, holding on to it tightly. Gemma did less well. She slid around in the saddle, lost hold of the reins, leaned forward and ended up almost hugging Arthur's neck. Without any instruction from her, he stopped in his tracks and she sat up again, red-faced. I wasn't sure if that was from embarrassment or joy.

"OK, all stop, since Gemma has. Just pull the reins a tiny bit, Martha, and Tim'll halt. That's right. So, how was your first trot?"

"A little scary," said Martha. "He joggles so much."

"Once you've gotten the feel of it, it's easy," he said reassuringly. "Let's have another try."

"With stirrups this time?" I suggested.

"Yes, but don't try to rise yet."

We walked, trotted, walked and trotted again till Martha and Gemma felt comfortable. Mr. Butler looked at his watch.

"That's enough for now," he said. "I'll show you how to rise to the trot tomorrow, you two, but you won't find it hard now that you're used to the pace. Now, back to the yard, I think."

Gemma and Martha watched Mr. Butler demonstrate how to rub the ponies down when we got back. Gemma was looking interested and involved, but Martha was jumping around as if she was cold.

"How are you doing?" I asked her.

Martha shrugged. "It's OK, I suppose."

OK? It was my turn to be open-mouthed. A morning riding Tim out in this glorious countryside, learning how to mount and sit and even to do sitting trot, and it was just OK?

Martha obviously realized I was feeling disappointed so she quickly added, "Tim's sweet. Thanks again for letting me have him. And I liked riding. It's just all this."

With a sweeping arm, she indicated the busy scene. Everyone was untacking ponies, rubbing them down, checking hoofs for stones, carrying saddles and bridles over to the tack room, leading ponies down to the paddock. How could anyone not enjoy all that?

"Which part in particular?" I asked weakly.

"Hefting saddles and things around isn't much fun, and I don't like having to clean him up."

"Groom him," I corrected her. "Well, I did tell you …"

"I know, but it didn't feel real before. I just want to go indoors and have some food."

"So do we all," I said, "and I desperately want a shower. Cheer up, Martha. The first day's always hard when you don't know the routine, but I bet by tonight you'll be having a fantastic time."

She nodded and started grooming Tim with the dandy brush Mr. Butler passed her, but I didn't get the feeling she was convinced and, to be honest, neither was I.

Still, we got indoors eventually. Megan and I took turns having showers and then took our dirty clothes down to Mrs. Butler who promised to get them washed and dry. Meanwhile I put on jeans. I noticed that Martha had already done the same thing, though I wouldn't have taken off jodhpurs for anything if I'd had them my first time.

We sat around the table eating a late lunch and talking noisily. Megan and Martha were next to each other, and I wasn't sorry not to have to talk to Martha. I found myself between Natalie and the smaller of the Ellies, the ones who were going to get their own ponies. Natalie was very knowledgeable and I thought she seemed a bit bossy. She was always tossing back her long red hair and saying what she thought. Ellie was sweet, very small and bouncy, a bit like her pony, Poppy, in fact. We spent a long time discussing exactly what qualities they'd need in a pony, and by the time we were eating fruit and cookies I'd forgotten about Martha's lukewarm attitude and was looking forward to the afternoon's activities.

But there was half an hour's free time first, and as Martha had disappeared I felt entitled to go off with Megan.

"I want to see Campbell," she said. "Do you know where he is?"

"Mr. Butler said he's got laminitis. That's serious, isn't it?"

"I don't really know. We'll have to ask. Well, he's not in the paddock, and he's not in Captain's stable. How about the far end of the yard?"

There was a wooden building there that I'd hardly noticed before. It had a stable door, and when we looked inside we found it was divided into two compartments, each of them lined with straw and each containing a pony. One was Campbell, who'd carried all the things we needed for the camping trip last summer – tents, food, water, cooking equipment, everything. He was almost black, with a long black mane and tail, like a much sturdier version of Bramble, and he stood looking rather miserable in one corner of his stall. We leaned over the door and chirruped at him, and he looked up, but he didn't bother to come over.

"Do you think we can go in and talk to him?" I asked.

"I don't see why not. We weren't told not to."

We opened the door and shut it behind us carefully, though I don't think there was much danger of Campbell trying to escape. He was standing rather oddly, as if he was trying to put all his weight on to his back feet, so that he looked skewed backwards. He seemed pleased to see us, and we spent a while stroking and patting him. Megan had brought a carrot with her, and we broke it into two bits and took turns feeding them to him. He looked more cheerful after that, though he had a perfectly good hay net hanging up so he couldn't have been hungry.

Someone yelled our names and we realized that the half hour was up, so we kissed Campbell's soft nose and told him we'd be back later. It was only as we were closing the door that we remembered that there was a second pony in the adjoining stall, so we had a quick look.

There couldn't be any doubt – it was the pregnant pony,

Snowdrop. Her tummy was enormously swollen, and she stood in a sort of daze, munching a mouthful of hay, and gazing at us in a bemused kind of way. We stretched over to pat her but didn't try to go in.

"I wonder if that's how you feel when you're waiting to have a baby?" speculated Megan. "Outsized and overwhelmed!"

"If it's her first, maybe she doesn't even know what's happening," I suggested. "Maybe she'll wake up one day and find she's a mother and wonder how it happened!"

That made us laugh and we were still giggling when we joined the others milling around in the yard. Martha looked across at me – and she was scowling.

45

Chapter Five

"Hey, Jess, come over here!"

There was space between Mike and Chris on the big sofa under the window and Mike was patting it invitingly. I felt myself go pink as I wandered over as casually as I could. Slanting rain was hurling itself against the windows and the world outside looked infinitely unwelcoming, in complete contrast to the cozy common room. The first part of the afternoon session had been outside. Mr. Butler had explained about keeping ponies out to graze all year round – how they need extra food but are all right for warmth as long as they're allowed to grow their own thick winter coats.

I don't think any of us was all that sorry when it started to rain and Mr. Butler told us to get indoors and meet in the common room in ten minutes, especially as the rain turned to a downpour almost instantly.

So I squeezed in between the two boys, feeling the draft from the bay window behind us and snuggling down into the soft cushions for protection.

"How was the ride this morning?" I asked. I was very conscious of them as boys, far more than I had been a year ago. I didn't really know why, it had just happened. I found myself thinking about Phil and comparing him with Mike.

Phil was tall and freckled, with gingery curly hair. Mike was tall too, and very thin. He looked like he was always bursting with energy, even when he was sitting down doing nothing. His hair was dark brown and spiky, and his face was pale and could look sharp and spiteful. Not now, though. He was smiling in a friendly way and behaving as if he wanted nothing more than to talk to me.

He started to describe the group ride, but we soon had to stop as Mr. Butler called for quiet.

"I know we're here to learn but don't we get any space?" Mike grumbled, quietly.

"I know," I agreed, "he doesn't believe in letting anyone waste time."

"I wouldn't be wasting time," he said, grinning slyly at me. He really was very likeable. I looked away, embarrassed, and caught Megan's eye. She winked at me and looked as if she wanted to giggle.

"OK, everyone, as we're indoors we'll focus on indoor pony management. Who can tell me some differences between keeping a pony at grass and in a stable?"

You know how it is when a teacher asks the class a question and everyone's seized by a kind of group embarrassment? That's what it was like. We all stared at our feet, or at the fire, and you could just feel the common desire not to speak and risk looking stupid or, worse, overeager.

"Come on!" said Mr. Butler, impatiently. "You're supposed to be interested in horses. This isn't school, you know!"

I delved around for something sensible to say, and had just opened my mouth when Natalie and Megan both started speaking, and after that the session was fine. Lots of stuff about the different types of bedding available – apparently you can get shredded paper nowadays which is ecologically better than straw, but if I had a pony I'd want straw because of the fantastic smell. And we had to work in groups to choose the best food for a stabled pony from a long list. I wanted to include lots of oats and corn but Chris said he thought they should be rationed as otherwise the pony would get too fat, and it turned out he was right.

"What about salt?" asked Martha, who seemed a lot happier now that we were indoors. "I'm sure I read somewhere that ponies need salt, but we're always being told too much salt's dangerous."

"Well, you're right," said Mr. Butler. "The best thing's a salt lick."

"What's that?"

"A block of salt hung up in the stable. Then the pony can have a lick whenever it likes."

"So we don't need to go and grind it over the food like one of those pizza waiters with pepper mills?" asked Megan.

"OK, that's enough for the moment," said Mr. Butler, through the laughter. "I think I've lost you for now. It's nearly supper time, anyway."

Later on, after a happy, laughing meal and a mammoth game of Monopoly, Martha and Megan and I took hot chocolate and cookies up to our room and snuggled under the comforters to talk. The curtains were open so that we could see the stars – the rain had stopped and it was going to be a cold night. We could hear voices drifting from the other rooms, and a door slammed from across the yard as the boys went into the cottage where they slept.

"D'you think Gemma's OK all on her own?" said Megan.

"We could ask her if she'd like to join us for a while," I suggested.

"I suppose we should."

"She's just very shy," said Martha. "I don't like to think of her all alone."

Megan went over to Gemma's door and knocked but there was no reply. She poked her head around the door and there was no one there, but she went on to the two Ellies' room and found Gemma already there with the four friends, looking a little lost but not left out, so that was all right and we three could relax.

Megan and I told Martha about our adventures on the last trip. Maybe we exaggerated a tad – anyway, by the time we'd finished Martha was looking really scared.

"I'm never going to be able to ride like you two," she moaned, "and tomorrow we've got to trot and go up and down properly."

"Don't worry!" I said. "We've all been there; it seems so scary and once you can do it you realize it's easy-peasy."

"That's not what you said after your first time," said Martha.

I'd described the first vacation in minute-by-minute detail to Martha, and I'd probably built things up a little too much. I shot a glance at Megan for help.

"Think about what fun it's been so far," she said sensibly. "Nothing awful happened today, did it?"

"It was all right," said Martha, cautiously. "I liked it when we walked back to the farm but I didn't much like going around and around in circles for ages."

"But that's schooling!" I said incredulously. "You're so lucky to be getting it. My first time I had to learn as I went along, but you've had a proper riding lesson!"

Martha sniffed and looked unconvinced. A cold feeling crept over me. What was it going to be like if Martha hated being here? It wasn't as if I could ignore her. OK, I hadn't exactly invited her to come, but I'd been so enthusiastic about riding for the last year that I had to take some responsibility. In fact, I knew perfectly well she'd never have come if it hadn't been for me.

"Well, I think we're all tired and ready for some sleep," said Megan, practically. "First days are always tough, Martha. Think about your first day at school, or doing anything new. There's so much to take in and it's worse if everyone else seems to know exactly what they're doing."

That cheered Martha up. We said goodnight and switched off the main light, and the breathing of the other two soon slowed with sleep.

"It's snowing!" Megan shook me. I rubbed my eyes and sat up. Streaks of white were flying past the window. We scrambled over to look out.

"It's not sticking," I said, sadly.

"Not yet, but it might later. Imagine, riding through snow! It'll be magical!"

"As long as they let us. Is it safe for the ponies?"

"I don't see why not. We might have to go slowly, and I bet we won't be out long, but just think …"

A picture of myself cantering Bramble through drifts of crisp white snow made me feel so excited. We grabbed each other and danced around in ecstasy.

"What's up?" Martha's tousled head emerged from a cocoon of warmth and she blinked at us in amazement.

"It's snowing!" we sang out.

Martha dragged the comforter with her over to the window and looked outside.

" 'Snot sticking," she said briefly, and went back to bed.

She had to get up soon anyway as it was time for breakfast. Afterwards, Caroline told us to wrap up warmly and meet her in the tack room, but she then disappointed us by saying we weren't going to ride till the weather improved.

"It's not fair," someone grumbled. "Why can't we?"

"Because of the wind chill," Caroline explained patiently. "Have some sense, all of you. We can ride out when it's cold, even in the snow, but at the moment the wind's so strong that the temperature's way below freezing and you'd be wishing we hadn't gone out within about two minutes."

"Are the ponies all right if it's so cold?" I asked, suddenly thinking of them shivering and wet in their exposed field.

"They'll be fine. They're designed to be out in all weather. If you went over to the paddock, which I don't suggest you do just now, you'd probably find them all huddled together for warmth in the most sheltered spot, against the hedge, I'd expect. They create their own heat by sticking together."

I still thought it was mean to leave them outside when it was so cold we weren't even allowed to be there at all, but on the other hand there wasn't much I could do about it. Caroline said we were going to clean tack for a while. It's a job I enjoy. There's something very satisfying about rubbing leather and metal till they shine, and it warms you up, too. The tack room was cold, but by the time we'd finished we were boiling.

Mike brought Bilbo's tack over to where I was sitting and we gossiped as we polished. He was being really nice and he was always so good at making me laugh. Most of his jokes were about the others – he had a real talent for watching people and finding what was funny about them. Ellie, Ellie, Sarah and Natalie were all together, talking about their lives at home, and Megan, I noticed with sudden pleasure, was talking with Chris, who might be a few months younger than we but was nice-looking and outgoing, just like she is. That left Martha and Gemma, who were sitting with Caroline being given a lecture on how to clean tack. It looked as if Martha was happier than yesterday. I went over to grab a can of saddle soap and said, "You OK?" and she smiled and said, "This is fun."

I was a little confused. How could anyone think cleaning tack was more fun than riding – well, unless the person you were with was something special? But if Martha was happy, then I didn't need to worry about her, so I smiled back and took the saddle soap over to Mike. He and I were starting to seem like special friends.

Later on we went indoors and watched a video about show jumping. Then the sleety snow had stopped and the wind had dropped by the time we'd finished lunch, and Mr. Butler told us we could ride. There were whoops of joy as we scrambled into our thickest clothes and ran across the damp yard to the paddock. The sun was shining and steam was coming off the ponies' backs as they warmed up. They mostly had their heads down, eating great clumps of hay from the scattered bales, but when we arrived they seemed happy enough to be caught and led up to the paddock fence.

I hoisted Bramble's gleaming saddle onto her glossy back, bent under her to do up the girth, and pulled the stirrups down the leathers, ready to mount. She tossed her head excitedly, whinnying, eager to get out for some exercise.

"Just hang on a minute, beautiful," I murmured to her, as I ducked under her head to fix the trailing halter rope, tucking it under her throat lash and checking that nothing was too tight. I didn't want to chafe her skin when it was so cold.

Next to me, Martha was struggling to finish Tim. I helped her with the bridle and showed her again how to check the girth with three fingers.

"Up you get," I said, holding Tim steady from the opposite side and pulling down on the right stirrup so that the saddle wouldn't shift as Martha got on – that's always discouraging when you're a new rider.

She remembered to position herself properly and hauled herself into the saddle, but she sat down with a hefty thump that made Tim sidestep. That made her lose balance, and she kept on going, slipping sideways out of the saddle and landing right on top of me. We flumped down together in a groaning heap on the hard concrete and, inevitably, everyone started laughing.

We picked ourselves up. Martha was all right, since she'd been on top of me. I was the one who'd had the hard landing. Still, I wasn't going to complain. The last thing I wanted was to give Martha any cause for moaning, so I grinned cheerfully and told her to try again.

I think she'd have quite happily given up and gone indoors, but everyone was watching so she had no choice

if she didn't want to look like a wimp. She went reluctantly
back to Tim's left side, put her foot into the stirrup as if she
was climbing Everest, and made a feeble hop, which got her
nowhere at all.

"I can't do it!" she wailed, sinking back onto the ground
and looking as if she might be about to burst into tears.

"Oh yes, you can. Put your knee here, in my hands."
Before she had time to draw breath, Mr. Butler had given
her a leg-up and she was in the saddle, wobbling but central.
Quickly, I pushed her right toe into the stirrup as Mr. Butler
did the same for her left. He caught my eye and winked
conspiratorially before looking up at Martha and telling her to
hold the reins properly and sit up straight.

Giggling to myself, I mounted Bramble and got her ready. She was a pony who liked to stretch her neck a lot, I'd discovered, so she was sometimes hard to hold. The reins were continually flexing between my fingers and even if it hadn't been cold I think I'd have needed the gloves or I'd have had blisters. Tim had tried to snatch mouthfuls of grass all the time when I'd started, but once I'd gotten the reins short enough he'd been willing to do what I wanted. I had the feeling that Bramble was eager and enthusiastic but a lot more headstrong than Tim.

Megan trotted across the yard and neatly halted Star next to Bramble. The two ponies obviously liked each other; they sniffed and touched noses and just seemed comfortable together. We were near the gate leading out to the lane so we'd be first when the ride started.

"Brrrr, it's freezing," said Megan. "My hands and feet are turning to blocks of ice."

"Me too," I said, "but don't say anything too loud. I don't want to discourage Martha any more."

Megan looked at Martha, who was sitting very stiffly on Tim, exactly as Mr. Butler had positioned her.

"It's a pity she's getting such cold weather for a first riding vacation, though," she said quietly. "It'd even discourage me if I didn't already have the bug."

I leaned forward and stroked Bramble's warm soft flank. Her skin shivered under my hand and her ears lifted and she stamped a foot impatiently. She was dying to get started and so was I. The weather didn't matter to me. As long as I could ride I didn't mind being freezing cold or soaking wet.

Megan was watching me. "Yeah, you really do have the bug," she said, sympathetically. "You could get to be a really good rider one day, you know."

"Some hope! I get two weeks a year if I'm lucky. No way will I ever get to be like those riders we saw on television this morning."

"Well, maybe not like them ... Is that what you'd like?" Megan sounded surprised, as if it wouldn't have crossed her mind that we could ride like professionals.

"More than anything, but there's no point even thinking about it. Some dreams just have to stay dreams."

"One day, when we're grown up, we could buy a place in the country together and keep horses there," Megan said, her eyes shining at the thought.

"That'd be magic. I'd have a gray, I think, a good show jumper."

"What I'd really love would be a jet black horse. It'd be very elegant and stylish and I'd keep its mane clipped and braided all the time, and I'd have really elegant tack."

We both went quiet, losing ourselves in dreams of imaginary horses.

"Time to get going!" called Mr. Butler, breaking into our reverie. "Jess and Megan, lead on and turn the other way toward the village. Then take the bridle path on the left, OK? The rest of you, follow in single file – if anyone's out driving this afternoon, they'll have enough to do on these narrow lanes when it's slippery without meeting ponies all over the place. Keep the pace up, girls, but don't trot."

Caroline opened the gate for us before mounting Blaze who was waiting patiently and placidly by her side. Megan kicked Star forward and I pressed my heels gently against Bramble's sides and then squeezed the reins slightly to tell her to follow. She stepped delicately through the gateway and I steered her left before she had time to follow Star automatically. If Megan thought I had it in me to be a really good rider, I wasn't going to waste my time being carried around. I was going to ride properly, all the time.

Chapter Six

The steady beat of hooves on the hard pavement gave way to
a soft padding noise, broken by the occasional jingling of a
piece of harness. We led the column along the road for a while
and then onto a narrow path that snaked between humps and
hollows of woodland. I vaguely recognized the scenery from
the first vacation, but it all looked so different in the depths
of winter. The pale sunlight shone through the bare branches
almost without interruption, but in the spring it had been
filtered into dappled shade by the thick covering of young
leaves. Those very leaves were now trampled underfoot,
providing the soft muffled carpet that the ponies were quietly
picking their way along. It was all incredibly peaceful and I
felt very happy, riding a gorgeous pony, my friends around
me, and still nearer the beginning than the end of the week.

Then Mr. Butler's voice sailed over the riders and ponies.

"Trot on when you're ready!"

Megan, in front of me, sat firmly into the saddle, let her
hands go forward a little to give Star her head, and kicked
gently. Instantly, Star responded by speeding up into a trot.
During all that, I was trying to keep ahead of Bramble, who
was eager to trot and inclined to start regardless of whether I
told her to. Slightly to my surprise, I was able to hold her back
in a joggy walk for a few seconds before applying the same

aids as Megan had. As soon as she had the signal, Bramble leapt forward into a fast trot and, thank goodness, this time we could rise and fall properly, after yesterday's uncomfortable sitting trot.

As I fixed the reins and concentrated on posting – that's the real word for going up and down when you trot – I could hear Mr. Butler's voice somewhere behind us, encouraging and instructing. Presumably he was helping Martha and Gemma at the back, and I vaguely wondered if Martha was enjoying herself more than yesterday.

Then there was a scuffling sound behind us, and a thump, thump of speeding hooves, and Chris came past me, maneuvering Rolo neatly between the trees, going at an impossibly fast trot. He hissed "Go, go, go!' as he shot by, and a second afterwards Mike came up behind me so that I was sandwiched between them. Bramble pulled enthusiastically and the reins whipped through my fingers. Her pace changed as she flattened into a canter at the same moment that Rolo and Bilbo did the same. Megan looked around, startled, saw what was happening, grinned and, turning back, leaned forward and kicked Star on. We were all four cantering now, and I could hear the thud of fast hooves behind me as well as some shouting and what sounded like a scream. Too late to worry about that, I thought, focusing on keeping my seat, on guiding Bramble along the narrow path, and on not letting her stumble into a hidden rabbit hole. I managed to pull Bramble back to a trot and risked a quick glance behind me as Bilbo overtook us, and saw the two Ellies, Natalie and Sarah, all accelerating toward me. I couldn't see the beginners, or Caroline or Mr. Butler, but who cared? This was great. I got myself balanced, shook the reins, and let Bramble enjoy herself.

"Heads down!" came a shout from in front, and I ducked automatically as a low branch whistled overhead. There was a cry behind me and I swiveled in the saddle to see Sarah sailing off Meg and landing in a pile of leaves. A part of me was thinking, I hope she's all right, but it was such a great ride and I knew someone would help her. Then, as we thundered along the path, another shout came back, "Log!" This time I was able to yell the same message behind me before I saw the tree trunk lying squarely across the path. It loomed up ahead, and my stomach turned over in a twisting sickening sensation, and then we were there. Bramble lifted her front legs and then her back and we were over without any effort from me, and then Bramble was stopping of her own accord among the other sweating, circling, happy ponies. A moment later we were joined by Poppy, Twinkle and Mr. Man with their riders, and by Meg, without a rider, her stirrups swinging wildly and her reins trailing dangerously to the ground.

"I'll catch her!" gasped Natalie, leaping off Mr. Man and throwing his reins into Ellie T's grasp. Meg had instinctively slowed when she came up to the other ponies, but she was still over-excited, snorting and prancing and generally making herself a nuisance to the others, and by the time Natalie took hold of the reins they'd been trodden on and the two loose ends were dangling on either side of Meg's neck.

"Whoops!" said someone. "Let's hope we don't get into trouble for that."

"What happened to Sarah?"

"She didn't get her head down in time," said Ellie P. "But I don't think she got hurt. It didn't look bad."

"I think that was me," I said, ashamed. "I didn't shout fast enough."

"Don't worry. At least we knew about the log in time," said Ellie T. "And it was a wicked ride."

We all agreed. Just then, Caroline came into view, cantering Blaze fast.

"Log!" we all yelled, but she drew him to a halt on the other side and looked across at us.

"Is Sarah all right?" asked Megan.

58

"She's fine. She didn't actually get into contact with the branch; she reacted by swinging away from it and that unseated her, and she landed in a great big soft pile of leaves. She'll be along in a second. So what happened? I don't remember anyone telling you to canter."

We all looked around at each other and instantly entered into an unspoken alliance.

"The ponies just got a little carried away," suggested Mike, innocently.

"Maybe they thought they heard someone say canter," said Natalie.

"I might have lost control," I volunteered, knowing I was still one of the least experienced riders.

Caroline looked around at us and raised her eyebrows.

"Well, I can see I won't get a real answer, so let's just presume there was a misunderstanding," she said.

There was a general sigh of relief when we realized we wouldn't be scolded.

"How did Martha and Gemma do?" Megan asked.

"They panicked a bit – did you hear Gemma screech? But luckily we were both concentrating on them, so we were able to help them take control. I came on ahead to make sure you bunch hadn't disappeared into blue smoke. Look, here's Sarah."

Sarah arrived first, her blonde curly hair disheveled, but perfectly cheerful. She took Meg's reins from Natalie and knotted them together before swinging into the saddle.

"Are you OK?" someone whispered, and she whispered back "Yes, don't mention it again; Mr. Butler doesn't know."

"He'll have to, I'm afraid," said Caroline in a normal voice, "but we won't make too much drama out of it. You *are* OK, aren't you?"

"It was nothing," Sarah said airily. "I just feel like a fool."

"No headache?"

"The branch didn't actually hit my head; I might've caught

the edge of it. I was already half out of the saddle, and it was just too much. Honestly, I didn't feel a thing and there's nothing wrong with me."

By now the others were joining us and Caroline assured Mr. Butler that we'd all stayed in control – which was more or less true, after all – and that the only fall hadn't been serious, and his frown lifted and everyone relaxed again.

"Well, I was going to suggest a canter anyway, so we'll let that one suffice," he said. "And Martha and Gemma are getting the hang of trotting now, so let's carry on. Take it gently over the stream, everyone."

We all nodded and got ready to set off again.

"Jess," said Mr. Butler, quietly.

"Yes?"

"You know Bramble doesn't like crossing water very much?"

I remembered the various occasions when I'd watched Phil persuading her.

"Yes, but she does go across, doesn't she?"

"Um, but you need to ride her positively. Push her on and she won't even notice till she's halfway through."

"OK."

I gathered the reins more tightly and settled well down into the saddle, keeping my back straight and my lower legs parallel to the stirrup leathers, so as to be sure to be able to control Bramble. She didn't like me holding her reins so tightly, and pulled and tossed her head till I gave her a little more movement, but I hoped I'd done enough. I could see the water ahead – a wide, shallow stream, glinting prettily in the sun. The water ran fast among chunks of stone and bits of tree trunk, making little waterfalls and deeper pools. The first ponies were already crossing, slowing down as they dropped their heads for a quick drink, and then kicking up water in sparkling showers as they clambered out the other side. I kept Bramble at a slow walk, so that we wouldn't be held back by ponies drinking, and by the time I got to the edge everyone else was on the other side and they were all watching me. Not what I'd intended!

"That's it, Jess!" called Mr. Butler encouragingly.

I blushed, feeling stupid. He didn't need to make me look like a novice; I'd crossed millions of streams on Bilbo and Tim, and we'd even cantered along the edge of a lake while we were on the camping trip.

Bramble paced slowly forward, till her foreleg touched the water, and then she stopped. A dramatic shiver ran through her body. I pressed my heels against her and then kicked a bit more strongly, but she refused to move. Quickly, before anyone could offer to come and help, I turned her back up the path a few paces, and then walked her steadily down to the stream again. Again, she stopped. I tried again, this time

putting her into a trot, but it just made the refusal even more dramatic. She leaned away dramatically and tossed her head, and for an awful moment I thought I was going to fall off.

The others were calling encouragement from the opposite side and no one seemed to be laughing, but I still felt silly. I didn't remember Phil ever having this much trouble with her.

"Jump down and lead her," advised Mr. Butler. "Or if you'd like, I'll come back over and give her a whack"

"No, don't," I called. "I'll do it."

I turned her and backtracked a little before slipping off Bramble's back. I stood by her for a moment, patting her and telling her she'd be fine. Then I pulled the reins over her head and twisted them around my right hand while holding them close to her bit with my left hand. I clicked at her and said, "Walk on!" encouragingly and she paced next to me as far as the water's edge.

I could feel her tensing up as we got close and sort of holding her hoof above the water for a split second, but then she put it in and we were starting across. I felt so pleased with myself that I forgot to keep such a tight hold and concentrated instead on choosing the best stones to step on. She was still following, but she must have suddenly realized where she was. Her head tossed up, my hold was too loose to keep a good hold on the reins, she stumbled dramatically on a loose stone and a heavy hoof landed excruciatingly hard on my left foot.

I screeched with pain, and at the same moment she pulled away and scrambled out onto the bank – luckily, in the direction we were going. That left me teetering on a wobbly slab of stone, with one foot in agony and the other waving about in the air, and icy water on all sides. There was a frozen second when time stood still. I could see everything – the other riders clustered open-mouthed opposite, the ponies watching Bramble, the black and gold woodland, and the pale sky … Then everything started again. I twisted so that my good foot could land on the slab; Mike leapt off Bilbo and rushed into the stream to grab me and between us we got out with no worse than a splashing.

Bramble shook herself theatrically and put her head down to snatch some grass. She'd had her little drama. Supported by Mike and Megan, I hobbled over to a convenient tree stump and sat down.

"Let me look at your foot," said Mike, resting my foot on his knee and pulling the boot off gently.

"Ouch!" I yelped, but despite the pain, I realized he was being especially solicitous toward me. Once my sock was off, everyone crowded around to look. I expected to see my toenails wrenched off, or bits of bone sticking out of my foot, but, slightly to my disappointment, everything looked quite normal, and actually it wasn't hurting that much. Mr. Butler took hold of my foot and flexed everything, and said it was only bruised, so I put my sock and boot back on and tried standing up. Mike insisted on putting his arm around my shoulders to support me, and Megan hovered by my elbow, but I didn't really need help any more.

"Are you OK to ride?" Mr. Butler asked.

I nodded.

"Good. Well, we've had a busy afternoon, but we need to be back before dark, so we must be off. Everyone get mounted."

It was dusk when we got back to the farm. For the last few yards along the road, Caroline held a lighted flashlight at the head of the column, and Mr. Butler did the same at the back. The farmhouse lights glowed warmly and invitingly, and we untacked and turned the ponies out at record speed, longing to be indoors by the fire, hungry for supper and hot drinks and, in my case at any rate, a long, hot bath.

But my plans for a cozy evening didn't exactly happen.

The first part did. I soaked away the ache in my foot and joined the others for a good meal and then we watched a movie. Mike seemed to want to be near me all the time but I wasn't so sure I wanted to ignore everyone else to concentrate on him.

Chris and Megan were sitting together in a corner, but Mike kept trying to detach me from the rest of the group, and when we were on our own he made lots of cutting remarks about the others – they were funny and quite often true, but it all started to feel a little unkind. At first, they'd all been strangers but now they were becoming our friends. Also, I was feeling bad that I hadn't spent much time with Martha, so eventually I told him I had to talk to her and went over to where she was sitting with Gemma, slightly apart from the rest, as usual.

"How's it going?" I said, sitting down next to them.

"Fine," said Gemma. She still sounded shy but her eyes were shining. "I love the ponies and I really feel I'm learning to ride."

"What was the best thing today?"

"The stream, definitely." I must have reacted because she added quickly, "Oh, not because of what happened to you. I just loved it when Arthur walked through the water. He wobbled a lot but I didn't feel like I'd fall off. And I can trot properly now – well, most of the time."

"That's great! Martha, what about you?"

I had a horrible feeling that Martha wasn't going to be so enthusiastic. I was right.

"It's all right, I suppose," she admitted in the most lukewarm voice. "Tim's sweet."

"But you don't really love it?"

"No."

"Not even being able to trot? Just think, you couldn't do anything yesterday morning and now you can ride!"

"So what?" she said, almost rudely. "It's only riding."

"But …"

"And it's not much fun being the beginners when everyone else can go galloping off into the distance all the time."

"It's all my fault," I said guiltily. "I went on and on about how fantastic it was. I should have told you more practical stuff. I feel really bad now."

64

"Don't – it's not your responsibility."

"But I could give you some tips …"

"Jess." Her voice was icy now and she stood up and looked down at me almost threateningly. "Don't you dare patronize me."

She stalked out of the room leaving me open-mouthed. Was I patronizing her? All I was trying to do was be friendly and sympathetic. Should I run after her? I could see everyone else watching me and I thought, there was enough of that this afternoon. So I sat down next to Gemma and tried to look as if what Martha had said really didn't matter at all, and the interrupted conversations in the rest of the room slowly resumed as people realized the show was over.

Gemma was looking at her feet again. I'd figured out that was what she always did when she felt uncomfortable.

"So what do you think of Arthur? I've never ridden him," I said, encouragingly, and that got her going. Once she got over being shy she was all right, not very exciting but nice, and the fact that she'd fallen in love with riding meant we had something in common. I told her a few stories about my other pony vacations and she explained how she'd always read about ponies but never had a chance to go riding, very much like me, really, and although it wasn't the most interesting half hour of my life, it was all pretty pleasant.

But inside I knew I'd have to deal with Martha soon, especially as we'd have to keep on being friends – or at least knowing each other – back in our regular lives. And I just didn't know what was the best thing to do.

We all went up to bed soon afterwards. The boys hung around gossiping at the farm doorway for a while, till Mrs. Butler came along and told them to move to the cottage, and Megan and I climbed the stairs wearily. My foot was aching again.

Martha was sitting on her bed, fully dressed, listening to music. She didn't look as if she was enjoying it. When she saw us, she moved to face the wall and turned the volume up so high that we could hear exactly what she was listening to, even through her headphones. Megan caught my eye and made a face. I shrugged back. It was such a ridiculous situation. No one wanted anyone to be unhappy. No one could make Martha enjoy riding if she didn't. No one could say, I hoped, that I hadn't been a good friend to her.

Except, of course, that I *had* spent a lot of time with Megan and Chris, and especially with Mike.

Megan went off to the bathroom and when she came back I went, and still Martha hadn't turned around. I got into bed and said, "Night," in a general way, but only Megan replied.

I lay in bed and worried. I wished I could phone home and talk to Mom, to get some advice. We'd switched off the light, but I could just make out where Martha sat huddled against the wall, and I could still hear her music. I lay very still, and after a while she turned it off and got ready for bed.

But it was obvious she didn't want to have anything at all to do with me.

Chapter Seven

I must have dropped off to sleep because when I next looked at my watch it was three o'clock. Something had roused me. I immediately thought of Martha's sulking, but when I looked at her bed there was no movement and I could hear her steady breathing, and on my other side Megan was snoring slightly. Maybe that had woken me? I snuggled back under the comforter and settled down again.

A minute later there was a strange groaning noise and I knew at once that was what I'd heard before. I sat up and listened intently, trying to work out where it came from. Was it one of the girls in another room? Maybe someone was ill? But the next time the moan came I realized it was from outside. I squashed my face against the window, trying to make out where it could be coming from. The paddock was way over to the left and I was pretty sure the noise was coming from the right. I opened the window to hear better, and an icy draft whistled into the room. Megan stirred and sat up.

"Shut the window!" she whispered. "It's freezing."

"I know, but listen."

The moaning noise drifted across the yard toward us again.

"Spooky," murmured Megan. "What d'you think it is? The ghost of Christmas Past?"

"It's really weird. Listen again."

We waited for a while, shivering. The noise didn't happen and I was just about to give up and close the window when we heard it again, fainter this time but still definitely there.

"It's not from the paddock," I said.

"Nor from the house. What about the boys' cottage?"

"I'm sure it's further away than that. Anyway, whoever it was would've woken the others by now, and there'd be lights on."

We leaned out as far as we dared. The cottage loomed, black and unlit, against its backdrop of trees.

"Well, if it's not them … what else is over there?"

"Captain's stable … and the stalls we found the other day. Campbell and the pregnant mare, what's her name – Snowdrop."

The moan rose and fell again. It wasn't that loud; I could see why no one else had been disturbed.

"It's got to be one of them," Megan said decisively. "We'd better wake Mr. and Mrs. Butler."

"Yes ... or we could go and take a look first ourselves. It might be nothing, and we'd have woken them for nothing."

"And much more fun. Hang on; I've got a flashlight here somewhere. We'd better put some clothes on, too."

We closed the window and drew the curtains back so there'd be a little moonlight. I could just make out the pile of clothes I'd taken off earlier. While we were stumbling around in the half-dark, trying to dress quietly, Martha woke up.

"What's up? Is something wrong?"

"Shhh!" I hissed and Megan whispered, "There's a strange noise coming from the yard. We think one of the ponies may be ill and we're going to investigate." There was a pause. Then she added, generously, "Do you want to come, too?"

"Sure."

Martha scrambled into her clothes. The three of us crept out of the room and downstairs. The door was bolted but I'd opened it very quietly in the past, when Rosie and I had gotten up extra early, so I knew how to draw back the bolt with minimal noise. We closed it gently behind us and tiptoed across the yard, aware of the bedroom windows just above us. Once we were clear of the main yard, we relaxed a little and switched on Megan's flashlight.

"You know what, I haven't heard anything for the last five minutes," remarked Megan.

"Me neither. Maybe whatever it is has stopped or gone to sleep."

"Good thing we didn't panic and wake up the Butlers, then."

"And anyway, this is wicked fun," added Martha.

We stopped with our backs to the tack room. Captain's stable was in front of us, and beyond that was the wooden building where we'd seen Snowdrop and Campbell on Monday.

"Well, there's no point standing around here in the cold,' said Martha, practically. "Let's check out the possibilities."

She strode over to Captain's stable, which had one of those doors divided into a top and bottom half, and unbolted the top. Megan pointed her flashlight inside and we could see Captain standing easily, leaning to one side, blinking sleepily.

"Not much wrong there," commented Megan.

"It's much more likely to be one of the other two," I said. "Campbell's got laminitis, after all. Maybe it got worse."

We carefully closed Captain's door and moved on to the stalls. The smell of hay mixed with pony manure hit our nostrils as soon as we went in, but it felt warm and welcoming even in the dark.

"Is there a light?" asked Megan, waving her flashlight.

I found a switch and turned it on. Campbell, straight in front of us, looked peaceful enough; he was standing almost exactly where we'd seen him before, with his sore hoof raised slightly so he wouldn't have to put any weight on it, but he didn't look at all distressed.

"Well, that just leaves Snowdrop," said Martha.

We looked into the second stall. Snowdrop was lying

down, and as we watched she bent her head around and tried to nibble her sides.

"What's she doing?" said Megan.

"Maybe she got bitten by mosquitoes?" I suggested.

"It's too cold for mosquitoes," Martha said. "And the other ponies would be doing the same, wouldn't they?"

"D'you think her sides hurt because they've stretched so much? I know when my Mom was pregnant with the twins, she had to use tubs and tubs of moisturizer."

"Well, you're not catching me smoothing baby oil onto her; she's far too big!"

"I didn't mean we'd have to, though I don't really see why not. Snowdrop, don't do that! You'll make yourself bleed!"

"Maybe she's going to have her foal," Martha said.

"No, Mr. Butler said it'd be a long time …"

As we watched, Snowdrop hauled herself up clumsily. She didn't come over to us or even seem to notice we were there. Instead, she started to pace around the stall, swishing her tail and stomping her feet, looking dangerous, so when she came past the doorway we instinctively stepped back. She kept looking intently at her sides and snapping at them, as if they were irritating her terribly.

"I think you're right; she *is* in labor!' said Megan. "Or if not, there's something really wrong. Colic or something."

"I'll run and get Mr. Butler, OK?" I offered.

"No, I'll go, I've got the flashlight."

Megan whizzed out of the door. Martha gripped my arm tensely as we watched Snowdrop.

"Can't we do something to help her?" she asked.

"I don't know. I don't think I've ever read anything about mares giving birth. I know a lot about foals."

"You would." She glanced at me and smiled suddenly. "That may come in useful later."

"Martha, I didn't ever mean to patronize you. I just wanted to help."

70

"I know; it's me. I had all these ideas about being a natural at riding. I'd seen myself leaping on a horse and going straight for a six-foot fence. Once I started, I realized it's just as hard as anything else you start."

"Harder than a lot of things, because it's not just you doing it. So much depends on the pony."

"Yes, and don't think I'm not grateful to you for letting me have Tim. When I watched you trying to drag Bramble through that river this afternoon …"

"It wasn't exactly a river. And you'd have been OK. Someone would've helped you."

"Yeah, well, maybe I don't like having to ask for help." She sounded quite fierce.

I tried a different tack.

"Well, you're getting better at the basics, and I know the weather doesn't help, but are you enjoying some of it?"

"I like all the social stuff, getting to know everyone. It's been a good time. But riding? It's not for me, I think."

I looked at her, feeling almost as helpless as I was where Snowdrop was concerned.

"Don't become a control freak, Jess," she said, gently. "Even though we're friends, we don't have to like the same things. And don't jump to extremes, either, and start thinking I'm having a terrible time. I'm all right, OK?"

Just then, Snowdrop, who'd been pacing around and around during all this soul-searching, stopped right by us and produced an almighty groan. She sort of pulled her lips back so that her chunky teeth showed right down to the gums, and Martha understandably took a big step back.

"Help!" she squeaked.

"It's not us," I said. "She's in pain. If only I knew what to do to help her."

Martha smiled ruefully. "Well, don't look at me. Nothing I know's going to be much use."

"What's keeping Mr. Butler? We should've woken him up

71

at the start. If something happens to Snowdrop just because we wanted an adventure, I'll never forgive myself."

"Calm down, Megan's hardly had time to get to the house yet. Look – what's she doing?"

Snowdrop seemed to be concentrating. Her tail was raised unnaturally high and she was swaying from side to side. Suddenly, in a quick swoosh, her legs were covered with a stream of liquid.

"Oh my goodness, what's happening?"

"That's gross!"

We clutched each other in fascinated horror as the liquid slowed to a trickle. Snowdrop started moving around again and, a few seconds later, she lay down.

"Should we do something?" Martha whispered, horrified, as the mare began biting her sides again.

"What? I don't know. Mr. Butler must be here soon!"

I was feeling really panicky now. Was something awful happening to Snowdrop?

Martha tore herself away to look through the door.

"They're coming!" she called.

There was a swift crunch of footsteps and then Mr. Butler was there, his bathrobe pulled on over sweat suit pants, with Megan scurrying behind him.

He stood and looked carefully at the pony lying straining on her straw bed.

"OK, girls, this is it. She's having her foal. The next thing we have to wait for is for her water to break, and then it'll take about twenty minutes."

"I think it already broke," I ventured. "At least, something happened."

"When?"

"While Megan was getting you … five minutes ago? She was standing up and all this stuff came out of her."

"That was it. Not all of it; with luck, the foal'll still be encased in a nice warm wet bag."

He looked around at us.

"Are you all OK? Not too cold?"

"We're fine," we chorused, though actually I was wishing I'd put some more clothes on. No way was I going to miss this.

"Jess, go and tell my wife it's definitely labor and have her call the vet. She's in the kitchen."

I borrowed Megan's flashlight and sprinted across the yard. It was weird being back in normality. The farmhouse was dark, but once I got to the kitchen the lights were on and it was warm and cozy. I could hardly believe that out there in the stable Snowdrop was fighting to bring her foal into the cold world. I delivered the message breathlessly, but Mrs. Butler seemed unfazed by all the drama.

"I'll get on the phone while you take these extra coats; you'll all freeze, out there in the middle of the night. Tell Dave I'll be along in a moment with hot drinks."

I nodded and ran back with an armful of assorted coats, wondering how she could be so calm. Back in the stall nothing much was happening. I wondered if the dramatic part had finished, and felt sorry Megan had missed it, even though it had been fairly disgusting. We hung around, leaning over the door and talking quietly. Mrs. Butler arrived with a thermos and some mugs and a steaming bucket of soapy water. Mr. Butler sponged Snowdrop gently and then joined us to drink hot cocoa gratefully, while Snowdrop lay on the straw, straining and groaning quietly and still occasionally snapping at her sides as if flies were biting her.

"Isn't there anything else we can do to help her?" asked Megan, after one particularly violent strain that made us all feel the mare's pain with her.

"No, this is how it should be. Foals are big creatures, and it's a big job getting them out."

"Will Snowdrop be OK?"

"There's no reason to think she won't. How long will Andrew be, Judith? That's the vet, girls."

"He'll be along when he can, but he's at another farm further along the valley. A difficult lambing, they said."

"At the moment there's not much he can do here, anyway. We just have to let nature take its course."

It seemed mean to be standing warm and wrapped up, while Snowdrop suffered in front of us, but Mr. Butler seemed to know what he was talking about.

"Should we wake the others?" I said suddenly. "They'll hate having missed this."

"That's a kind thought, but I think Snowdrop'd prefer having fewer spectators," Mrs. Butler said. "In fact, if this goes on much longer, I think you three ought to get back to bed."

She looked around at our open-mouthed horror and

relented. "All right, but don't blame me if you're exhausted tomorrow. This could go on for a while yet."

"No, I think things are moving along," said Mr. Butler, interrupting. "Look!"

Snowdrop had lain down with her head toward us, but if we crowded to one side we could just see her hindquarters, and there, suddenly, we could see something new. A sort of slimy bubble was growing in front of our eyes, and in it I could just make out a shape.

"What is it?" Martha whispered, awed.

"It's the foreleg, but still in the amniotic fluid, the bag of water that half broke earlier. That makes it less painful for Snowdrop, d'you see? Now, girls, stay safely on this side of the gate. I'm going to go in with her again and see if I can help."

"Be careful!" squeaked Megan, thinking of how violently the mare had been nipping at herself earlier.

"Don't worry, I think she's got other things to worry about than me at the moment."

Mr. Butler opened and closed the gate quickly and knelt down beside Snowdrop, stroking her side rhythmically and watching her intently.

"Won't be long now," he reported quietly.

Sure enough, a few seconds later Snowdrop gave a convulsive heave, grunted dramatically, and the slimy bag stretched further. I thought I could glimpse a head in there – were those ears?

It's going to die, it can't breathe in there, I thought agonizingly. *Why doesn't Mr. Butler do something?*

Then something even worse happened. With the front of her foal literally hanging out of her, Snowdrop suddenly scrambled to her feet, and stood straining and sweating. It was revolting, fascinating, terrifying, and beautiful, all at once. We stood silently, clutching each other, as the mare tottered around in a circle and then collapsed onto the floor again, this

75

time with her back toward us. Mr. Butler, who'd stayed very still while she was on her feet, knelt down again by the half-born foal.

"Come on now, girl," he muttered. "One big push and it'll be out."

Snowdrop gathered herself visibly for a terrific effort. She strained and pushed – and the foal was born! Its shoulders came out and Mr. Butler leaned forward and broke the bag over the foal's head so it could breathe. From being a repulsive something in a slimy bag, it instantly became a gorgeous baby creature, its eyes tightly shut, its long nose whiffling as it smelled the new world around it, its ears already starting to lift from their position close to the head. Mr. Butler quickly lifted the whole messy package – foal and bag and yucky stuff – so that Snowdrop could reach it, and she immediately lowered her head to inspect this damp stranger. We watched, fascinated, as she sniffed and nuzzled and licked her baby, cleaning its eyes and nostrils and making lovely soft whickers and whinnies, as if she was talking to it and welcoming it into the world.

It was by far the most amazing experience I had ever had. I wanted to cry and laugh at the same time.

"Well, girls, that's a sight not too many people get the chance to see," said Mr. Butler, standing up and wiping his hand on a wisp of straw. "She'll do fine now. That's a nice little girl foal she's got there."

He came out of the stall and washed his hands in the bucket of water.

"Time to get back to bed, girls," said Mrs. Butler.

"Oh, but ..."

"No buts," Mr. Butler confirmed. "I'll wait for the vet to get here and have a look, but everything's fine. By morning she'll be up and moving around."

"Snowdrop?"

"No, the foal."

76

He smiled at our incredulous expressions.

"That's why they give birth at night," he explained, "so that predators can't attack while they're vulnerable. She'll be suckling milk in a while, and able to run in a few hours."

"Wow!" I breathed, remembering how helpless my baby brother and sister were for months after they were born. "Aren't ponies cool?"

"Amazing," agreed Megan.

And Martha, who'd started the night so anti-ponies, said, "Totally and utterly amazing."

Chapter Eight

When the three of us crawled down to breakfast, heavy-eyed and yawning, everyone was talking about the foal, and the girls had already been to see her.

"She's actually standing up!" breathed Sarah in an awed voice. "Just imagine, four hours after being born."

"And she's drinking from her mother. She has to lean under, she's got such long legs," added Ellie T.

I remembered how those legs had been twisted tight so she could make it out of her mother.

"What color is she?" asked Megan.

Ellie P stared at her. "Weren't you there? We heard you saw her being born."

"Um, but she was still all wet when we got shoved off to bed. She could have been any color."

"I think she'll be like her mother, dappled gray," said Natalie. "You can't really tell about her tail and mane yet, though, cause they're tiny. Her tail's about six inches long."

"How's Snowdrop?" I asked.

"She seems fine. What was it like when she actually gave birth?"

We launched into a detailed description of our exciting night, while the others listened and commented and envied us. The boys were less entranced than the girls; they looked

78

a little nauseated and then pretended they were bored and wandered off to the common room.

"Where's Mr. Butler?" I asked, when we'd covered every possible angle. "Is he still in bed?"

"I don't think he went to bed," said Natalie. "He told us the vet came around dawn to make sure all was well, and that's not long ago. In fact, we heard his car, and that's when we woke up and realized we'd missed all the excitement."

"Not that the boys were so excited," commented Ellie T. "We woke Gemma up so she could come and inspect the foal with us, but the boys weren't even interested enough to get out of bed."

"Typical," grinned Megan. "I've got two brothers. I know what they're like!"

"You were so lucky, you three," Gemma said, shyly, and Martha started telling her all about it again.

Mrs. Butler came in to see if we'd finished eating.

"What are we doing today?" I asked.

"Well, it depends," she said. "Dave's going to need a bit of rest after being up all night, so Caroline's in charge. There's a lot of snow forecast. Not just sleet like the other day, so if there's any riding to be done, it will have to be this morning."

"Snow!"

We all looked at each other with shining eyes. Up here in the hills, we'd get real snow, not just the slushy icy stuff but deep and crisp and even. We crowded around the window, peering out at the steely clouds and wondering when the first flakes would fall.

Caroline bustled in, full of excitement about the foal.

"She's going to be a real beauty," she promised. "Snowdrop's a pretty mare, and her daughter will be better still. Whoever buys her will be very lucky."

"Won't she stay here?" I asked.

"Probably not. She'll be here for a few months, of course,

while she's still suckling from her Mom, but I doubt if Dave wants to bother with breaking her in."

"What's that?" asked Martha.

"That's the process of training her to be ridden. Getting her to wear a saddle and bridle, and learning to behave properly. It's quite a complicated business."

"But isn't she wearing a head collar already?" asked Sarah.

"Yes, just a lightweight one. It's called a slip. It makes her easier to handle," Caroline explained. "Especially as we'll be turning them out into the paddock before too long."

"Surely it'll be too cold for her?"

"We'll wait till it warms up a bit, but these are native ponies. They're bred for the climate and it's not good to treat them too softly."

"And how long will it be before she can be ridden?" asked Megan. "For instance, if Mr. Butler does decide to keep her here, would one of us be able to ride her next year?"

"Maybe when she's two, more likely when she's three," Caroline replied. "I doubt if she'll be ready for use as a trail riding pony till she's three, but she'll be lunged and all that much earlier."

"It's all so complicated," Martha complained. "I wouldn't have thought it was all that hard to teach a pony how to be ridden. After all, if we can learn to ride in a couple of days, why doesn't it work the other way around?"

Caroline laughed. "For all sorts of reasons, one of which is that ponies are a lot stronger than you are, and if they decide to do what they want, your riding skills wouldn't be much help. But the other thing is that it takes a long time for them to be strong enough. They're born with long legs so they can run away, but they're much too delicate to be ridden."

I gazed out of the window and imagined owning the new foal; schooling it, looking after it, and eventually riding it. How cool it would be to ride a pony you'd broken in yourself!

"Can we go and see them now?" I asked, breaking in to the conversation.

"What? No, sorry, Jess. No more visits today. Mr. Butler doesn't want them disturbed."

That was disappointing, but there wasn't time to think about it as Caroline said that if we wanted to ride we'd have to get a move on. She said it would be very cold, and that anyone who preferred not to ride could stay behind, and, hardly to my surprise, Martha said she'd stay indoors and help Mrs. Butler with the lunch. Gemma, on the other hand, was as eager as the rest of us, and both the boys, when we tracked them down by the video game again, said they'd ride.

We got into our warmest clothes and went out to catch the ponies. The air was icy and got into your throat right away, but the clouds had lifted a little and there was even a glint of sunshine. The ponies were all huddled together at the bottom of the paddock, but they seemed happy to be going out. Tim looked surprised that no one was catching him, so I gave Bramble's halter to Megan and asked her to lead her up to the yard while I gave Tim some much-needed attention. We spent a contented five minutes together. He was still my favorite pony, even though I didn't ride him any more. His soft gray nose whiffled adorably as he allowed me to stroke his head, and his mane was so fine it almost floated when I ran my hands through it. I gave him a carrot, which he ate solemnly, looking at me earnestly while orange driblets dropped from his mouth to the ground. Then I gave him a good hug, and left him to have a peaceful morning.

Megan had collected my bridle as well as hers, so it didn't take me long to catch up with the others. Soon we were all ready. The ponies were stamping and tossing heads and jiggling around; I'm sure they needed to keep warm as much as we did.

"Gemma, I want you at the back with me," ordered Caroline, holding Blaze in as he tried to circle impatiently.

"So we need someone sensible to lead. Mike, you can go first."

Mike winked at me as he maneuvered Bilbo past. I was amazed that Caroline had chosen him. He was always the one setting up trouble, even if it had all been harmless this vacation. But then he was also very good at pretending none of it had anything to do with him, and Caroline was nowhere near as good as Mr. Butler at detecting mischief. I got Bramble to follow Bilbo as we set off down the lane at a steady walk. We went into the field where we'd done the schooling the first day, and onto the steep track.

"Can we trot?" Mike called back to Caroline.

"Yes, but absolutely no cantering!" she yelled back. "Remember, Gemma's with me!"

It was much warmer once we were in the woods and trotting. The regular up and down movement got our muscles working and we had to concentrate, too, on holding the ponies in. Maybe it was the cold weather, but they all seemed to be fidgety and straining to go faster.

I let Bramble go up parallel to Bilbo. "I wish we could do something a little more exciting than all this trotting. We're all capable of some jumping, for instance."

"As we proved yesterday with that log. But you're right. I want to do some real jumps, but maybe they think it's too cold."

"Can't see what difference that makes. There are a few logs alongside this path later on. Let's have a shot at those."

"Will Caroline let us?"

"Will she know?"

I turned in the saddle. The line of riders stretched back up the hill. It looked as if some people had slowed down to a walk; no one was near us and Caroline and Gemma were nowhere to be seen.

"OK, let's go for it. Where do we find these logs?"

"Just around the corner. Come on, quick."

He shook Bilbo's reins and made a clicking noise. Bilbo responded by trotting faster.

"She said we can't canter," I said breathlessly, as Bramble followed Bilbo's lead.

"And you want to be good?"

I nodded, though that made me feel silly. Fortunately Mike didn't seem to mind.

"So we won't canter. All you have to do is keep rising and sitting, and not let her have her head too much, and you can go almost as fast at a trot as at a canter."

It was true, though it was really hard keeping Bramble back. She kept lurching forward into canter and having to be pulled back into trot. My arms were aching and so were my leg muscles when we wheeled around the final corner and saw the junction of the two paths.

"Around to the left," said Mike. "Just follow Bilbo and me."

I grabbed the saddle for a moment as we swung rapidly onto a grassy area next to the track. It stretched away for a good distance, shaded by big trees but free of undergrowth, and there were regular clusters of tree trunks that must have been cut down and left there for collection later. Some of them were individual ones, but mostly they were in groups.

I pulled Bramble into a walk, though she danced around excitedly.

"Hey, Mike, this looks kinda hard. D'you think the ponies can manage all this?"

But he just looked back over his shoulder as he moved Bilbo toward the first log and called, "Come on, scaredy cat!"

Bilbo went for the jump eagerly, kicking up his heels and trying to go for the next, but Mike steered him around to face me and halted.

"Come on!" he urged impatiently. "I thought you could jump."

"I can!"

I pressed Bramble's sides and she responded with a rapid trot that became a canter as we approached the log. I forgot all the stuff I'd learned in the past about adopting the correct position for jumping, and just sat a bit forward and let myself go with the jump. She made a massive leap and landed heavily, almost shaking me off. I lost both stirrups and nearly lost the reins, but I remembered instinctively to grip hard with my knees and I also grabbed a handful of mane to steady myself. If Bramble had decided to keep going toward the next jump I couldn't have prevented her, but luckily she stopped next to Bilbo and put her head down to have a mouthful of grass. That was the last straw as far as my balance was concerned, and I slipped over her shoulder and did a forward roll onto the ground. I managed to hang onto the reins, though, and as I picked myself up I was able to laugh with Mike rather than feel embarrassed.

"So who cantered?" he teased, moving Bilbo so he could help me steady Bramble.

"Yes, well, it wasn't my telling her to," I countered, shoving my foot into the stirrup and trying to remount. Bramble wouldn't stay still and I had to hop around after her even though Mike had grabbed her noseband.

"Try now," he said, and I made another jump and this time just managed to get aboard, though my legs were telling me they were really tired. I couldn't think why. Unfortunately, Bilbo decided that he'd had enough and took a nip at Bramble, who stepped back quickly to avoid his snapping teeth. Mike was still holding Bramble's noseband and maybe not bothering too much about his own pony – anyway, the next thing that happened was that he fell off between the two ponies, although his right foot was still caught in the stirrup.

"Get Bilbo!" he shouted. I leaned forward but Bilbo was stepping away. Mike was on his back, trying to detach his foot, but the angles were all wrong. So I slid off Bramble, and ran over to grab Bilbo's reins, and fortunately he let me take him. A moment later Mike was standing up and brushing himself down and we had both ponies back under control.

"Are you OK?" he asked, putting an arm around my shoulders.

"Um, fine," I said, not sure whether to show I'd noticed his arm. "Thanks for helping me."

"Thanks for helping *me*," he countered, smiling at me. Our faces were very close …

We'd gone the wrong way and had to catch up to the others, but Caroline didn't seem to mind. She just said she was glad we hadn't gotten lost, as it would start snowing soon, and told us to hurry up with the ponies, as lunch was ready.

She came up to me when I was in the tack room, though, and said, "Everything all right?"

"Yes, except I'm really tired after last night. Why?"

"I had a vague feeling you had a bit of trouble with Mike last time you were both here. I just wanted to make sure."

"We're getting along fine," I reassured her, touched that she'd remembered. "In fact, very fine."

She laughed and patted me on the shoulder.

Megan and Martha put me through practically the same conversation after lunch, when we were talking in our room.

"You can't blame us for worrying," Martha said defensively. "After all, you told both of us about how he bullied you."

"I suppose so, but we did make up then. He's nicer now, anyway."

Megan and Martha looked at each other.

"Maybe," Megan said, "and maybe not. Leopards don't change their spots."

"He doesn't have any spots!" I exclaimed indignantly. "Not like Gemma."

"That's not very kind," remarked Martha. "She can't help them, you know."

"She could wash her hair," I said.

"She does. It's just one of those teenager things that you have to go through," Megan said. "We were talking about it this morning after you disappeared with Mike."

"Oh." I felt a little deflated. "I didn't mean to sound mean. I actually like her."

"How generous of you!" said Martha.

"No, I mean, she's nice. Mike's nice. Oh, for goodness sake, they're all nice!"

We all looked at each other and dissolved into friendly giggles.

"Are you tired?" asked Megan. "Cuz I feel like I haven't slept for a week."

"Me too," added Martha. "I keep yawning."

"That's a relief," I said. "I thought maybe I was getting sick. Do you think we're just exhausted?"

"We were up half the night."

"Why don't we try and doze for an hour or two?" suggested Megan. "We're only missing a video about dressage. We can always watch that another time."

"As if we'd ever want to," murmured Martha.

I actually would have liked to. But it was true that I felt incredibly tired and thought a nap would probably be best.

When we finally woke up a couple of hours later it was to see that a strange white light had filled the room. We ran to the window and looked out. Snow was falling fast and the yard was covered with a blanket of unbelievably beautiful, pristine, white fluff.

Chapter Nine

"Duck!"

A snowball landed on my back as I twisted away. Feverishly, I scraped together enough snow to form a large, soft, ball and aimed back at Martha. It exploded onto her woolly hat and showered over her. Skidding and sliding, she raced after me in a mad twirling chase and cornered me by the tack room.

"Revenge!" she cried, stuffing snow down my neck.

I screeched as the freezing water trickled down my back. "Get her!" I yelled to Mike.

He grinned and started making a giant missile. Martha saw it and ran for cover. I struggled to my feet, giggling and shivering at the same time.

"Let's take sides; war!" shouted Chris excitedly, sprinting over to us. "Us three against the girls!"

Even with all the excitement I was still flattered that he was treating me like one of the guys, but it seemed a little unfair to be three against seven, so I yelled to Megan and Martha to join us. There was a frenzied few moments while each side assembled as many snowballs as we could, and then someone yelled, "Go!" and we all started throwing. The air was thick with fluttering snowflakes as the snowballs hit or missed and disintegrated, and rang with laughter and excited screams. We ended up chasing each other, trying to catch anyone and stuff snow down their neck, giggling hysterically. It was the best fun.

Mrs. Butler called us in just as we were all starting to feel uncomfortably cold. She'd made delicious hot soup and we sat around the fire in the common room, holding steaming mugs in our hands. It was bliss.

"I wish we'd gotten to see the foal again," Megan murmured to me after we'd warmed up.

I looked out. "It's getting dark. I suppose we could go now."

"We were told not to."

I thought for a while. "We weren't told not to visit Campbell. I actually feel bad about him. I said I'd visit him at least once a day and I haven't."

"Well, I think we should make up for that, right away," said Megan, her eyes gleaming. "We'll need to slip away quietly, though."

"That won't be hard. There's sure to be time before supper. Should we get Martha?"

We looked at each other.

"Let's just go together. It'll be more fun," Megan said.

Half an hour later, we were tiptoeing across the yard. It was colder than ever and the snow, which had been soft and feathery, was getting stiff and crackly.

"Poor ponies, down in their paddock," I said.

"Mmmm. But they've got lots of extra hay, and the snow's not lying under the trees. They'll be all right. Better them than me, though. I'm glad I've got a warm house to sleep in tonight."

The stall was dark, but we'd brought Megan's flashlight. We slipped in and closed the door before turning it on, in case anyone was looking from the house. Campbell was looking a lot more alert than the last time we'd seen him. He wasn't standing strangely any more, and he whinnied at us and looked hopeful. We went into the stall with him and spent a few minutes making a fuss over him and feeding him tidbits. I'd managed to get some sugar lumps from the kitchen and he really loved those, crunching them greedily. We talked about the trip and how sweet Campbell had been as a pack pony. And Megan told me stories about him on her other vacations at the farm.

Eventually we gave him a last hug and closed the door firmly. There was a shuffling sound from the other stall, but it was too dark to make out anything till Megan shone her flashlight. Then we both gasped.

When we'd last seen the foal, she'd been a crumpled mass of soft damp fur and grunge. Now she was standing up, watching us, her head bent to one side quizzically, as if she was wondering who we were. Her legs were amazingly long, completely out of proportion to her body, and her knees were adorably knobby. Her coat was pale gray with little spots of darker color, and she had big brown eyes and the longest eyelashes, like something out of a cartoon. Megan gently held out a hand and chirruped softly. The foal's head tipped to the other side, making us both giggle. That seemed to rouse her mother, who was standing with her back to us, head down.

"It's OK, Snowdrop," I whispered. "We've only come for a look; we won't touch your baby."

Snowdrop relaxed as if she understood. The foal took a wobbly step toward her mother and bent her delicate neck so that she could drink from her. It was the most incredible sight.

"I think we should leave them alone," murmured Megan.

"Just a moment longer."

We watched, entranced, for a few more minutes. The foal finished drinking and then folded herself up into a lying position, suddenly tiny against her mother. Her head went down onto her front legs.

"Just like she was when she was born," Megan said.

"That's probably still how she feels most comfortable," I said. "I remember when Holly and Tim were born; they used to lie in the most peculiar positions for the first few weeks. As if they were still inside Mom, I suppose."

We tore ourselves away after that and closed the stable door quietly so as not to disturb the three ponies left inside. As we reached Captain's stall, the farmhouse door opened and Mr. Butler was silhouetted against it, holding a flashlight and talking loudly to someone inside.

"Help, he mustn't find us!"

"Get over here by the cottage!"

We stumbled in the dark toward the cottage where the boys slept. The snow glittered in front of us, but it was surprisingly hard to see exactly where we were going and both of us skidded about on the icy surface, trying to be as quiet as possible.

Mr. Butler stomped across the yard. He must have heard us because his flashlight beam swung around in an arc and caught us right outside the cottage.

"What are you two up to?" he called. "You haven't been disturbing Snowdrop, have you?"

"Oh, no," said Megan, managing to sound genuinely surprised. "We were just exploring."

"We never get snow like this at home," I added.

"Count yourselves lucky,'" Mr. Butler said. "I'd happily do without it. Well, supper's on the table so you'd better get a move on."

"Yes, Mr. Butler," we chorused, clomping through the drifts of snow that lay against the buildings and reaching the back door. He was still watching us.

"Is the foal all right?" I called, thinking that would make it seem less likely we'd been to see her.

"She was fine when I came by an hour ago. Suckling nicely. You can see her tomorrow."

"Thanks, Mr. Butler."

"And girls."

"Yes?"

"Thanks for all you did last night. It could have made all the difference between a healthy birth and a disaster. You did well."

He turned at last and went off toward the stable. We sighed with relief and went indoors to take off our wet boots and coats and join the others for supper.

"And don't forget," hissed Megan conspiratorially as I started to push open the dining room door, "we *didn't* go to see Snowdrop."

The talk was all of foals that evening, and the two boys got fed up and headed to their rooms early. Natalie found a book on the common room shelves, which explained all about horses giving birth with the most gruesome pictures, and we spent a long time studying it, comparing what we'd seen with the author's ideas. Ellie P announced that she'd decided she didn't want a grown-up pony after all, and that she was going to ask her parents to buy Snowdrop's foal and let her train it.

"It wouldn't be much fun not being able to ride it," Ellie T pointed out.

"I wouldn't mind," Ellie P maintained. "That foal's going to be mine."

Mr. Butler came in just then and overheard.

"You'd need a lot of time and patience," he said, "and, of course, it would rely on the foal being up for sale."

"Caroline said you won't keep her," said Megan.

"Well, Caroline might be wrong. I haven't made my mind up yet, but I think I might. I'll see how she progresses over the next couple of months. So, sorry, Ellie, back to the drawing board."

Ellie looked a bit sulky.

"What are we going to do tomorrow?" I asked, thinking it might be a good idea to change the subject.

"I think we'll give you a choice in the morning, but all indoor things. Then we'll see in the afternoon if it's OK to ride."

"It's fun riding in the snow," said Sarah. "I'm sure none of us minds getting cold."

"We'll see."

He wouldn't commit himself any further. Tomorrow would be Thursday – we were past the halfway point of the week. I thought back over the rides we'd had, and felt a bit disappointed that there hadn't been more. The theory had been interesting, of course, and maybe would be useful one day, but with only three more riding days available I hoped desperately that most of the time would be spent in the saddle.

Still, we had to be content with what Mr. Butler had said

and hope the weather would be fine. Next morning, I jumped right out of bed to look at the sky. It glittered blue and white. There had been no more snow, but it all looked very cold. Icicles hung from the eaves above the bedroom window, gleaming in the sun.

"Everyone up!" called Mr. Butler from downstairs. "There's work to be done before breakfast."

We scrambled into our clothes and all got downstairs just as the boys dashed in from outside.

"It's freezing out there!" said Chris, his voice muffled by the scarf he'd wound about six times around his neck.

"Yes, well, don't start taking your things off," said Mr. Butler, "and girls, you need to get coats on."

Puzzled, we obeyed and all clustered outside in the yard, the snow squeaky under our boots.

"Everyone take a bale of hay," Mr. Butler instructed us. "The ponies need extra rations while it's so cold."

We went over to the hay store, an open-sided barn, and tried to lift the bales, but they were ridiculously bulky and heavy. We had to take one for every two of us, except for the boys who didn't want to look like weaklings. We staggered into the paddock and skidded, giggling and clutching at each other, down the slippery slope to where the ponies huddled under the shelter of trees. Megan had been right – the snow hadn't gotten through to the grass there, and there was a comforting layer of hay scattered everywhere. But it was really cold and you could see the heat from the ponies rising into the air like a mist.

"Jess, see if the water trough's iced up."

The long, low metal trough was further out into the field. I touched the water surface tentatively, but it had turned into hard ice. I bashed at it with the side of my hand but nothing happened, so I looked around for something to break it with.

"Try this," said Mike, hefting a broken tree branch.

We lifted it together and thwacked it down onto the ice. The surface shot into an explosion of lines, but the ice didn't break.

"It must be about an inch thick,' said Martha, interestedly. Almost everyone had wandered over to watch.

I had another try, on my own, aiming at where the broken threads were. The surface quivered but nothing more.

"OK. Let me at it!"

Mike gestured for me to stand back and lifted the wood over his head. He crashed it down on the ice with tremendous force. The sheet of ice cracked, split, and toppled inwards and a fountain of water shot upwards and drenched him.

"Ouch!" he screeched. "It's freezing!"

"Too true," said Mr. Butler dryly. "That's what I call overkill. There are easier ways of breaking the ice, you know."

We watched open-mouthed, waiting to see if Mike would explode with anger. He never liked to be criticized, or to look foolish.

Dripping wet, he looked around at us, as if daring us to laugh at him. No one moved a muscle. A shard of ice that had lodged in his hat slid slowly down the side of his face and he flicked it away. Then he caught my eye and an irresistible urge to laugh mixed with a kind of panic bubbled up inside me. I had a sudden picture from the first vacation of me, covered in cow muck because he'd pushed me in, and of him bogged down in mud, because I'd tricked him there. And now, here he was rapidly turning into an iceberg and it hadn't been my fault, but he couldn't blame me, could he?

As if he read my thoughts, Mike's expression went through anger to questioning and then his mouth curled and a slow smile lit up his eyes.

And as if in answer, we all, including Mike, started to laugh, and the tension broke. The ponies, who'd been watching curiously, shouldered past and started drinking. When they looked up, their mouths dribbled little slivers of ice.

"You'd better get back to the house and get changed," Mr. Butler advised.

"OK." Mike was shivering now. He set off uphill at a run.

"Go on, Jess, go with him and make sure he's all right," Mr. Butler added, surprisingly.

I looked around at the others, shrugged my shoulders, and ran after Mike.

At breakfast, Megan and Martha cornered me.

"So?"

"What do you mean?" I said.

"So what happened?"

"When?"

Martha sighed. "When you got back here, of course."

"Oh," I paused. "Oh, nothing."

They looked disappointed but I concentrated on eating oatmeal and the subject changed.

Actually, "nothing" wasn't entirely true, as they'd guessed. I'd caught up with Mike as he was sloshing across the yard, and he'd grabbed me and given me a swinging, laughing hug.

"Are you OK?" I'd asked breathlessly.

"Definitely OK," he'd said, and then he'd planted a tiny kiss on my forehead and had disappeared into the cottage. I'd gone indoors and waited for the others, still feeling a little breathless, but no longer because of running uphill in the cold. And I certainly wasn't going to share all that with Martha and Megan; that was between Mike and me.

Mr. Butler divided us into two groups for the morning.

"It's too cold to ride yet," he said, "but hopefully the temperature will go up this afternoon. They're forecasting a thaw."

"That's a pity," said someone. "No more snowball fights."

"But more riding," said someone else.

"Exactly. Be ready to ride at two o'clock; wear lots of clothes, as it'll be cold and damp. When it thaws, we could have fog for a while. Now, for this morning. The reason

96

you're in two groups is so you can spend some time with Snowdrop. I don't want her frightened by too many people. So the first group can go down there with me in a minute, and the second group is going to learn about pony ailments. Then in an hour or so we'll swap. OK?"

We all nodded, though actually I was a little disappointed. Whether on purpose or not, Mr. Butler had separated Mike and me, and he'd also put Megan in the other group. I trudged through the snow accompanied by Martha, Gemma, Natalie and Ellie P, and wished I were with the others.

Still, it was great to see the foal again, though I had to remember to sound as if I hadn't seen her since she was first born. She was moving around quite steadily now, and she seemed braver, coming toward our outstretched hands and letting us touch her baby soft neck. Her face was delicate and innocent; somehow all big eyes and tender nose, and her little mop of a tail wiggled adorably whenever she drank from her mother. Snowdrop was much more comfortable and relaxed. Ellie was allowed to go in and give her a bucket of pony nuts, which she ate voraciously. Then Natalie and I were told we could give her a gentle grooming. We used soft brushes and she seemed to enjoy the attention, though Natalie was annoying, telling me what to do as if I'd never seen a body brush before. Martha and Gemma had to refill the water buckets from the tap out in the yard, and staggered in carrying it between them.

"Shouldn't we muck them out?" asked Natalie.

"Yes, normally you'd do that first, but the other group can do that."

"Oh, good," I said, looking around at the piles of manure scattered in the straw.

"But you can all muck out Campbell. Off you go."

We went next door to Campbell's stall. He was looking much better. Mr. Butler went in with us and lifted each of his feet, showing us how the front hoofs were hot and tender.

"Will he get better?" Ellie wanted to know, stroking his soft nose.

"It depends. If this is acute laminitis, it'll clear and he'll be back with all the others. But if it's chronic …"

"What happens then?"

"Basically, it means the pony won't get better. He'll have to be put down."

There was a stunned silence.

"Surely there's something that can be done?" asked Natalie.

"Well, as I said, if it turns out to be the acute form, he'll get better. We should know pretty soon. But otherwise, we have to make an unpleasant decision."

I hadn't ever really thought about ponies being ill or getting old. I'd read a dramatic story about a horse with colic once, which had sounded terrifying, but the horse had recovered. But that was in a story, and this was real life.

"Is he having any treatment?" I asked.

"The vet's given him an anti-inflammatory injection, but basically it's a question of patience. He mustn't go into the paddock for now, and he needs to rest a lot."

"And if he gets better, will he be out trail riding with the others again?" asked Gemma.

"Well, the trouble is, he may be sensitive to grass after this, so he may need to be stabled indoors, and I don't think that would work here. But don't worry," Mr. Butler added as Gemma's eyes filled with tears, "if worst comes to worst, we'll find him a good home. Now, girls, time to muck him out."

One of the advantages of most of the ponies living outdoors was that we didn't need to clean up after them, but Campbell and Snowdrop had nowhere to go but on the straw. Natalie jumped at the job of leading Campbell out of the stall and the rest of us trundled in a wheelbarrow and some tools. Then we had to shovel up every single dropping and, after shaking the straw clear, dump the mess into the wheelbarrow. Some of it was dry, but some lumps were hot and steamy, and there was a very strong smell that made our noses wrinkle.

"Fresh today!" caroled Ellie, forking a chunk onto the pile cheerfully.

"It's disgusting," moaned Martha, shielding her nose with her scarf. "Imagine having to do this every day!"

The rest of us looked at her but we didn't say anything. I was sure the others were all thinking the same as I; that nothing could be better than having a pony to muck out all the time.

Gemma volunteered to wheel the barrow outside and tip the contents onto the muckheap, while the rest of us spread clean, fresh-smelling straw on top of what was left. Then Natalie led Campbell in again. He was walking with a slight limp, but he seemed to me to be putting his weight more or less evenly on all four hoofs.

"What do you think?" I said to Mr. Butler who was watching the pony intently.

"It all looks hopeful, but don't count any chickens just yet. Thanks, girls. You've done a fine job. Get back to the house and tell the other group to come out, will you? Caroline'll be ready for you."

We strolled back across the yard, breathing in the clean, snow-scented air contentedly.

"I don't envy that other group," said Ellie.

"Why not?"

"Didn't you notice how messy Snowdrop's stall is? That'll be a lot yuckier to muck out. And they won't get the fun of grooming her, either."

"They'll do Campbell instead, I suppose."

"Which is OK, but not as much fun as being in with the foal. She's so cute."

"And," remarked Martha practically, "they've got two ponies to muck out instead of one. I'm starving – let's see if we can scrounge some cookies."

Chapter Ten

The rest of the morning was spent in the warmth of the common room, learning about some of the illnesses ponies get. Caroline told us about colic – a really bad stomachache – and ringworm, which gives the pony little bald patches and which humans can catch too, and all sorts of leg problems apart from laminitis.

By two o'clock we were all in the paddock again, muffled up in scarves and gloves, catching the ponies and bringing them in to be tacked up. Mr. Butler had been right about the weather. The snow was melting fast and the ground was soggy and squelched under Bramble's weight. She seemed eager to go out, though, and mouthed the bit eagerly as I slipped it in. My cold fingers fumbled with the buckles on her noseband and throat lash, but once I was mounted I could feel the warmth from her body under mine.

We followed the usual route out onto the lane and then into the big field where we'd done the schooling. The snow still lay in piles in places, and we had to help the ponies pick their way in between so they wouldn't get compacted snow in their shoes. Even so, they skidded alarmingly sometimes, and both Ellie T and Chris nearly fell off before we'd reached the woods. Martha and Gemma were going very slowly, both hanging onto anything they could reach – saddles, reins, manes – so as not to fall off.

Once we got into the woods we went in single file, very slowly, nothing like the fast pace I'd used on previous rides. The snow had almost melted here, but the ground was soft and the ponies stumbled and tripped. At the point where the tracks split, Mr. Butler led us left, past the logs we'd jumped.

"Can we jump over those?" called Mike from the back of the line.

Mr. Butler called a halt and we gathered together.

"It's up to you," he said. "With the ground like this, I wouldn't try anything high, but if you know how to jump, you could try the lower ones."

"Great!" said Natalie. "Me first!"

She tightened Mr. Man's reins and kicked him into a trot, circling back to where the first log lay.

"Hold on a second!" said Mr. Butler. "Let me make it absolutely clear which logs you can go for."

He cantered Captain along the track and came back toward us, pointing out five logs he thought would be safe to jump. Four were single ones, but the last was a double, though not very high. "You can do all of these at a trot," he advised. "It's slippery, so that's safer."

"I'm not jumping anything," Martha declared, holding Tim in unnecessarily tightly.

"Don't worry, you don't have to," Caroline reassured her. "Nor you, Gemma."

"I'd like to try," Gemma said, bravely.

"Not today while it's so slippery. We'll see if we can find an easy jump for you tomorrow. Wait over here with me."

The rest of us lined up behind Natalie and took turns at the course. It was great fun. Although I'd jumped Tim and Bilbo before, Bramble felt quite different, much bouncier, and I really needed to get into the proper jumping position. No wonder I'd nearly fallen off yesterday when I'd been unprepared. But provided I leaned forward in the proper position, looking between her ears, with my elbows in a straight line along the reins to Bramble's mouth and my rear end just raised above the saddle, she was great to jump, full of enthusiasm and energy. The only difficulty was to keep her from cantering, but on the other hand I felt good that I could control her and keep her trotting even when half the time we were flying through the air.

"Wow, Jess, I wish I could ride like that," said Gemma, as I drew Bramble up next to her after my turn.

"I've only just learned," I said, surprised. "We did a tiny bit my first week, but a lot more in August. I don't really know what I'm doing yet, though. You should've seen Tom on Rolo when we did the gymkhana. He was fantastic."

"Look, Chris is jumping him now," said Caroline.

We watched Chris kick the big, heavy gray into the fastest trot. Rolo soared over the logs, high enough to clear three times the height, and came back to us snorting and tossing his head. Chris leaned forward to stroke his neck.

"Well done, boy," he said. "You'd like more of that, wouldn't you?"

"Yes, but not this afternoon," said Martha, rubbing her arms energetically to keep warm. "The rest of us might freeze to death while we're waiting for you."

Megan completed the course as we were talking and came over looking pleased. She'd jumped Star beautifully – neat, controlled, balanced.

"That's how to do it," I told Gemma.

"I still think you looked best," she said obstinately.

Once everyone who wanted to had had a try, Mr. Butler and Caroline took Captain and Blaze over the logs. Captain barely noticed they were there; he just lifted slightly. Blaze, though, thumped toward the first log and stopped dead, almost throwing Caroline off over his head.

She sat back down and quickly turned him in a tight circle

so he approached the jump again almost before he knew it, but again he refused. Caroline went bright red. It must have been really embarrassing for her, the person who was meant to be an expert, not getting her pony to do what she asked.

"What's the problem?" Mr. Butler called.

"I don't know. He's supposed to love jumping."

"I think he's limping," said Sarah, suddenly.

Caroline slid off and pulled the reins over his head to lead him while we all watched.

"So he is! Good observation," said Mr. Butler.

Caroline ran her hand down each foreleg to make Blaze lift his hoofs. "He's cast a shoe," she said. "From his off fore. Drat! I wonder when that happened."

"Can you still ride him?" I asked.

"He should be fine as long as I go very gently. I'll stick to the shoulder up on the road."

Mike had ridden back up the tracks a few yards.

"Here it is!" he exclaimed, jumping off and picking up a horseshoe from a sticky, muddy patch. He led Bilbo over to Caroline and gave it to her.

"Good, we should be able to use that again," she said, examining it carefully.

"Can't you put it back on now?" asked Gemma.

"No, we need a farrier," said Mr. Butler, "but luckily we'd already asked him to come over tomorrow to shoe Magpie, so he can do Blaze at the same time. Now, I think we'd better split up. Caroline, you go straight back up through the field and take anyone who's had enough with you. What about you, Martha? Ready to go back?"

He smiled kindly at her and I thought how nice he was, understanding that she wasn't enjoying riding that much. Gemma said she'd go with them, too, and the two Ellies said they were getting very cold. So they all set off for the farm at a slow walk, and Mr. Butler looked around at the rest of us.

"All happy to go on?" he asked.

There was a chorus of assent.

"Let's be off, then!"

He swung back into Captain's saddle and clicked at him. The big horse moved smoothly into a controlled, composed trot, and we all fell into line behind.

"Who's at the back?" Mr. Butler asked, twisting in the saddle to see. "Chris – keep up with us. Yell if there's a problem."

"Will do!"

There wasn't much talking for the next half hour. The path went uphill and out onto the open field, where the snow was still lying in patches, and we had to pick our way through it, but we kept at a trot mostly and it was a great way to warm up. The only movement in the wide white and brown landscape was the line of ponies jogging along steadily, and the only noise was that of riding – jangling harness, the squeak of leather, and the thud of hoofs on soft ground. The sky merged into the horizon ahead, all misty gray, and we could have been a million miles from cities and school and ordinary life. It was magical.

Finally the path we were following led by way of a gate into the woods, and we slowed to a walk again. Mr. Butler called us to stop and give the ponies a breather. Some people dismounted but I stayed on Bramble, lifting my legs to make sure the girth was still tight and then leaning forward to hug her beautiful, strong, sweet-smelling neck. Her mane flicked cold against my nose, tickling. I was so happy.

"It's nearly four," Mr. Butler said, "so we need to get back. Stick close in line and be careful not to lose sight of it – there are lots of wrong turns in these woods."

He waited till everyone was mounted again and went around checking that we were all OK. Then he led off, followed by Natalie, then Sarah, Mike, Megan, Chris and finally me. The path was narrow so we had to stay in single file. We trotted, but Bramble seemed to be getting tired and kept dropping back into a walk. I called Chris, who turned, saw me struggling to push Bramble on, and waited for me.

"Problem?" he said.

"I don't think so. She's just doesn't want to trot."

"Maybe she's cast a shoe, too."

I dismounted and lifted each leg in turn. All of Bramble's shoes were safely in place.

"Try walking her to see if she's limping."

I led her up the path a way and turned back.

"I can't see anything wrong," I said, worried. "What do you think? I'd hate to ride her if she isn't well."

"We heard too much stuff about illnesses this morning," said Chris. "You're getting neurotic. All she's done is not want to trot. Get back on and see if she'll follow Rolo and me."

Chris squeezed Rolo's sides and the pony obediently started trotting. I scrambled on quickly and gave Bramble the aids to trot. She started but soon went back to a walk again.

"She's just not taking any notice of me."

"Give her a kick!' advised Chris.

I hate doing that, but everyone tells me it doesn't actually hurt the pony, and it did start Bramble going at a very slow trot. We jogged along after Rolo for a while, till we reached a point where the track divided and we suddenly realized that we'd fallen behind the others and had absolutely no idea which way they'd gone.

We looked at each other in dismay. It was getting darker by the minute, but what was really worrying was that the mist that had feathered along the horizon earlier had invaded the woodland and was rapidly becoming a blanket. Instead of being able to see a long way along both paths, the fog was limiting our vision to a few yards and, as we discovered when we tried shouting for the others, it had a horrible way of swallowing up sound, too. Now what were we going to do?

"They can't have gotten far. We only stopped for a moment," I said.

"Either way, we've got to make a decision. Do we stay here and wait for them to come back for us, or do we take a chance on the right path?"

"Maybe we can see hoof prints," I suggested, maneuvering Bramble around to examine the ground at the start of each path. Unfortunately, though, there were lots of scattered leaves, and where the ground was clear it was stony and didn't show marks. And anyway the fog was thickening so quickly it was getting hard to see anything more than a yard or two ahead.

"I think we should wait," Chris said.

I shivered. "It's freezing," I said. "Surely we'd be better off moving along?"

"Let's dismount and lead the ponies for a while. That way we might see some hoof prints."

So we chose the right hand path at random and started down it, watching the ground for prints and listening all the time for the sound of the others. We led the ponies. They'd picked up our tension and were jittery and reluctant to follow.

"This is no good," I said suddenly, stopping in a glade where the trees were further apart. "We should go back. If the others are on the other path, they'll never find us on this one."

"You're right. Let's go back. It's a little spooky, isn't it," he added, nonchalantly.

A little! I held my tongue, but inside my heart was pounding with fear.

We turned carefully but the fog was so thick now that we couldn't find the path we'd come on. We circled the glade in rising panic, checking any path that looked familiar, trying to make out hoof prints, and, of course, the more we did that the worse the confusion became and the less likely it was that we'd ever find the correct path.

"It's no good," I said, choking back tears. "I don't think we'll ever get out. I hate these woods!"

"Me too. Are you cold?"

I nodded. We huddled together, clutching the ponies' reins and trying to pick up some warmth from their bodies. They wouldn't stay still, though. They were both restless and moving from side to side.

"Settle down," I said to Bramble, a little impatiently, giving her reins a tug. "There's nothing we can do except wait."

But Bramble had other ideas. She pulled back from my hand, jerking the reins from my numb grip, and in a flurry of hoofs disappeared from our sight. For a few seconds we could hear her crashing along through the woods, and then the fog engulfed the sound. Luckily, we'd both instinctively grabbed at Rolo's reins as Bramble shot off and made sure he couldn't follow her.

"Don't let go!" panted Chris, untying the halter rope, which all the ponies wore, from its safe position tucked under the throat lash, and using it as well as the reins to tie Rolo to a tree. "OK, he can't get away. Now what?"

"We could stay here till someone finds us, I suppose."

"That won't be till morning. We could freeze to death by then."

"I don't think it's actually freezing any longer," I pointed out.

"Well, it probably will be by morning," he rejoined, sounding annoyed. "Think about it, Jess. It's been snowing for the last two days. It's hardly going to be hot enough to camp out."

"Well, what else can we do?" I'm ashamed to admit I did start crying at this point, though I tried not to let Chris see. Not that that was hard. Visibility was practically nil and I could only just see him silhouetted against Rolo's bulk.

"They'll send out a search party," he said, suddenly. "Of course they will. They'll get back to the farm, get flashlights and stuff, and come out after us. They know where we are, more or less."

This was a comforting thought although it sounded as if we might have to wait for a long time to be rescued. We slumped down onto a dryish log and sat squashed together. Everything went silent for a few minutes. I was stretching my hearing to the utmost trying to pick up anything useful, but the only sound was an eerie owl hoot.

"I don't suppose there are wild animals in these woods, are there?" I said.

"I don't think so." Chris reached out for my hand and held it comfortingly. "Mr. Butler's never mentioned anything bigger than badgers. Unless you're scared of rabbits, of course?"

It wasn't exactly a joke, but I appreciated his trying to lighten things up. I produced the best laugh I could and searched my brain in vain for something funny to say back.

"Mike really likes you," he said, out of the blue.

"Does he?"

"Come on, Jess, you know he does."

I felt a warm glow inside me. "He *is* nice," I said.

"I was thinking … you know Megan?"

"Yes." I waited a while for him to go on.

"I wondered if you knew if she might feel that way, too."

"About Mike? No, I don't think so. They get along all right, that's all."

"No, I meant about me."

"Oh. Oh, I don't really know."

"Oh."

There was another long silence. I squeezed Chris's hand.

"She probably does, you know," I said, thinking he deserved some cheering up. "Why not talk to her?"

"When we get back. Yes, that'd be good."

He sounded a lot less gloomy instantly. I just hoped Megan wouldn't let me down when we finally got back to the farm.

"I'll tell you about when we got lost last summer," I suggested. "Well, Megan and I didn't get lost, but the boys did, and we went half way up a mountain searching for them."

I told him the story in detail and he listened intently. When I stopped, the quietness and loneliness of the woods flooded straight back.

"Chris," I said very softly.

"Yes?"

"I don't like this."

"Me neither."

There was a long pause. Then he leapt to his feet and yelled, "Of course!"

"What?"

"Quick, can you get up on Rolo?"

"Well, yes, but …"

"Get a move on!"

"Why?" I asked, fumbling to reach Rolo's stirrups. "I can't actually get my foot in, Chris, he's too big."

"Stand on that log, then."

I scrambled onto the log and Chris pulled Rolo along so I could mount. As soon as I'd settled into the saddle,

still puzzled about what we were doing, Chris told me to slide forward and he vaulted up behind me. It was seriously uncomfortable as I was sitting almost on top of the pommel.

"Pass me the reins," he said, "and let me have the stirrups. You can hang on somehow, can't you?"

"I suppose so." Chris had passed the reins over Rolo's head and I'd been holding them tightly. Carefully, I passed them over my head so Chris could take them. Rolo took a couple of steps and I wobbled in my precarious position and slid back into the saddle, almost sitting on top of Chris.

"Watch out!" he said. "That hurt. Try and stay forward."

"I'll try, but I wish I knew why. What are we doing?"

"Riding Rolo, of course." He sounded surprised.

"Yes, but why? We're still lost and it's still dark."

"But Rolo might not be. Lost, I mean. Don't animals have an instinct for getting home? They don't need maps like we do. They just know. So if we let Rolo go exactly where he likes, I'll bet you anything he'll take us back to the farm."

He shook the reins and we both sat still, trying not to guide Rolo. I held onto the pommel and to Rolo's mane, and Chris kept his hands close by my sides, steadying me. At first, Rolo moved slowly and as if he didn't know where he was going, but after a while he strode out more purposefully, brushing through trees and following what seemed to be some sort of path, and almost before we'd dared start hoping, we realized we were on a real trail, going uphill which seemed right, and suddenly, there was the noise of hoofs, and voices calling, and flashlights piercing the fog, and there were Caroline and Mr. Butler on Blaze and Captain, looking extremely worried and breaking into happy smiles when they saw us, and we were rescued.

And all of it was thanks to Rolo's fantastic pony instincts.

Chapter Eleven

"No riding for Jess and Chris this morning," announced Mr. Butler.

I choked on my mouthful of bacon.

"Why not?" Chris challenged instantly. "Why us?"

"Cuz you caused all that panic last night, stupid," said Mike.

Chris punched him hard enough to make his chair fall backwards. The crash brought Mrs. Butler into the room.

"What's going on?" she said, sounding quite fierce. "Boys, get up at once. Dave?"

Dave Butler, who always seemed so authoritative with us, looked positively sheepish.

"He said Jess and Chris can't ride," said someone.

"It's not fair," said Megan, loyally, and everyone added their pleas, too. It was very flattering.

"Let me just get a word in edgewise," yelled Mr. Butler over the bedlam. "It was a joke, OK? I didn't actually mean it. Of course I know they didn't mean to get lost."

"And they behaved very sensibly, too," added Mrs. Butler, patting my shoulder. "Such a sensible idea, letting Rolo bring them back."

"That was Chris's idea," I murmured, not wanting to take credit for his initiative.

"Doesn't matter; you got back here and no one was hurt."

That was true. Apparently when the rest of the riders realized we were missing, it was already so foggy and gloomy they didn't search for long, but had gone right back for flashlights as we imagined they would. Then Caroline, Mr. Butler, Megan and Mike had started back, only to meet Bramble cantering home, in a bit of a panic, but uninjured. That got them worried, of course. Megan and Mike had led Bramble back to the farm, while the adults kept going, and not long afterwards they'd met us on Rolo. To our surprise, they hadn't been angry with us. Sarah, Natalie and the two Ellies had volunteered to untack and groom Bramble and Rolo while we had hot baths, and the evening had been spent peacefully playing cards in front of the fire.

"So, *are* we allowed to ride this morning?" I checked.

"No …'" Mr. Butler raised a hand to quell the instant protest, "because *no one's* riding this morning. See?" He still looked stern, and we looked at each other, puzzled. Had we all done something wrong?

"Why not?" someone ventured.

"Because we're having a long ride up into the hills after an early lunch," he said, relenting and grinning as we all sighed with relief. "And this morning should be very interesting. The farrier's coming."

"What's a farrier?" asked Martha, the only person who hadn't looked sorry when we thought we wouldn't be riding.

"Someone who shoes horses and ponies. Matt has a traveling forge. He's been booked in for Magpie, but I'll get him to do Blaze, too, and he'll probably take a look at Campbell. Farriers know a lot about lame ponies."

We all gathered in the yard to watch. Matt was young and very strong, and good looking too; none of us girls minded spending a couple of hours with him. The boys were naturally more interested in his van, which held his forge.

"Don't get anywhere near that," he warned. "It goes up to 2300 degrees Fahrenheit. That would burn you to a crisp in no time at all."

He put on a leather apron and turned his attention to Magpie, a lovely piebald pony that we'd only seen down in the field all week. She'd cast a near hind shoe – that is, the back left one. He lifted her leg and showed us the hoof.

"Look how uneven the edge is," he said. "I'll pare that away."

We gasped in horror as he took an enormous pair of metal pincers and started using them to cut off chunks of hoof.

"You'll hurt her!" someone said.

"Not like this. It's just like cutting your toenails. That doesn't hurt, does it?"

It was hard to believe Magpie wasn't in pain as the massive clippers worked around the hoof but she certainly didn't seem bothered. Once he'd finished, Matt used a metal blade like a massive emery board to rasp the hoof and make sure the surface was completely even. He showed us how he avoided the softer area, the frog, at the back of the hoof.

"Why do ponies have that?" asked Chris. "It seems like asking for trouble to have a soft part."

"It does have a function, though," said Mr. Butler. "Does anyone know what?"

"I do," Natalie said. "It's so they don't slip, isn't it?"

"Absolutely right."

Natalie looked pleased with herself. Mike whispered, "Know-it-all," in my ear and I giggled. Natalie was a bit of a smart aleck, sometimes.

"I don't see why horses need shoes at all, with all that hard stuff," commented Megan.

"Well, in a way it isn't hard enough. If they're only on grass, they don't really need shoes, but if they do any roadwork, the road surface wears down the horn faster than it can grow, so the frog gets exposed. So we reshoe every few weeks and tidy everything up at the same time."

Matt managed to explain all that while he was shaping a bar of red-hot metal which he then carefully lifted out of the forge. He slammed it onto an odd-shaped metal stand, the anvil, and bashed at it with a hefty hammer. Sparks flew off in all directions, but the metal changed shape with magical ease, twisting from a long rod to a three-quarters circle. Once the basic shape was set, Matt used pliers to twist up the edges. He explained shoes for hind feet have two clips to help hold them on. Then he made a groove along the underside and skewered little holes along it for the nails, and then threw it into a waiting bucket of water. Steam hissed up in billows. Almost at once, Matt lifted Magpie's leg again, resting her foot against his apron, and pressed the hot shoe against her hoof. Even though I knew that part of the hoof was hard and nerveless, it was painful to watch, especially when he started hitting long nails into the horn, but Magpie didn't move a muscle.

"Almost done," Matt grunted, looking hot and sweaty. "Just need to tidy up."

He made sure the nails were safe for Magpie and sanded away at any sharp edges.

"Now she's done. Good girl." He gave Magpie a friendly slap and told Ellie T and Sarah, who'd been holding her, to lead her back to the paddock.

Mr. Butler brought Blaze in next and Megan and I volunteered to hold him.

"We found the shoe," said Mike, holding it up.

"Great. Let's just check to see if it still fits. Any of you want to help?"'

Most of us held back. It was fascinating but it looked dangerous, too. I was glad to be occupied at Blaze's head.

Chris offered to help, though, and so did Mike. He never liked letting Chris do anything he couldn't.

"Don't stand where he can kick you; come from the side," advised Matt. "See if you can rasp off some new growth."

Both boys went red in the face as they worked.

"It's mega tough," Mike said, wiping his forehead. "I haven't been this hot all week."

Chris didn't say anything but kept his head down, straining to make a difference to the hoof.

"Let's have a look, guys. Hmmm. Not bad."

Chris and Mike looked pleased – till they saw how quickly Matt rasped off a lot more horn.

"How long does it take to learn to be a farrier?" asked Ellie T.

"You'll be surprised," said Mr. Butler.

"It takes seven years," said Natalie. "I've read about it."

Chris whistled. "Why?"

"It's a complex job," Mr. Butler explained, "and you learn a lot of different skills. Do you think you'd enjoy doing it?"

Chris looked thoughtful. "It's a good way to be around horses."

"It's a good life, all in all," commented Matt, straightening up and letting Blaze's leg drop. "But hard on the back! OK, you two, take him away."

Megan and I led Blaze to the paddock and let him go. He seemed pleased to be back with his friends, and cantered off with Mr. Man and Meg. We leaned on the fence and watched, as we'd done so many times before. The snow had all melted overnight, and you could imagine spring was just around the corner. A soft breeze blew in our faces and the sun on our backs was almost hot. The ponies had spread right out over the field now that they didn't need to huddle together for warmth any more. Most of them were grazing.

"I wonder when we'll be back next," I said idly, watching Bilbo sidle up to Twinkle and Arthur and wondering if he'd nip them. He didn't – he mostly kept his naughtiness for humans, and then only when he was bored. I liked Bilbo. I knew how he felt sometimes.

"Mom was asking my brothers if they'd like to have a vacation here," said Megan.

"That could be fun."

"Mmmm. I'm not sure if she meant I could come too, though. It's expensive enough for two."

"That would be really harsh," I sympathized. "The only thing is, it would give you time alone with your Mom."

Megan's father was dead and her Mom had to look after Megan and two younger boys alone. Whenever I got fed up with my parents nowadays, I tried to remember how lucky I was to have both of them.

"Sure," said Megan. "Good thinking, Jess."

I wasn't sure if she meant that or was being sarcastic, so I changed the subject. I told her about what Chris had said when we were lost.

"Whoops," said Megan, looking amused.

"You don't like him enough, then?" I asked tentatively. I seemed to be the lucky one where boys were concerned at the farm, but Megan was really pretty and deserved a boyfriend.

"He's too icky," she said. "Showing off all the time. Always has to be best. He should get together with Natalie."

"Soul mates," I said laughing.

"What about you and Mike?"

"It's nothing really," I said, going red. "Just a little fun. I'll never see him again, probably."

"Phil's going to be miffed when he finds out."

I shrugged. "He won't. Anyway, Phil and I are just friends. He texts me sometimes, that's all."

Someone shouted to us to go in for lunch.

"I think you've forgotten something," said Megan, starting across the yard.

"What?"

116

"Phil and Mike go to the same school, and I can't imagine Mike keeping quiet about his conquests, can you? Especially if he can stir up a little trouble."

I stopped in my tracks. I'd completely forgotten that. And now that I'd been reminded, I had absolutely no idea how I should react.

I sat through lunch in a daze. Chris and Mike were joshing happily with the four girls, and Martha and Gemma had their heads together discussing music. Megan joined in and left me alone to think. I liked Mike. I liked Phil. Neither of them was going to be exactly important to my life bearing in mind the fact that they lived miles away. Why shouldn't I be friends with both of them, and even flirt a little, as long as no one got hurt? That seemed to make sense to me.

"OK, let's get moving!" Caroline called. We bundled into our outdoor clothes – the sun had gone in and it was colder again – and whizzed outside to get the ponies ready.

Bramble trotted up to me as soon as I got into the paddock. "You clever girl," I said, stroking her velvety muzzle. "Let's have a terrific ride, OK?"

The procession of ponies clattered out of the yard and along lanes to the village. I remembered going there to buy a postcard and presents for my family last Easter. It all looked closed up for the winter, with no vacationers around, but there were still a few locals watching so I focused on sitting very straight and making sure my legs and arms were at exactly the right angle. Bramble was being very responsive and I found that if I kept my hands very low, almost touching her neck, the slightest movement transmitted my instructions to her.

"That's good technique," commented Caroline, trotting up along the column and reining in next to me.

"She's just being great this afternoon," I said.

"You can take credit for that. She's got a sensitive mouth for a trail riding pony, and you've found out how to use the aids properly. Well done."

117

Caroline kicked Blaze on to join Mr. Butler at the front and left me glowing with pride. I didn't look around to see how Mike behind me was taking it. I didn't want to disturb the perfect balance that I was feeling with my pony. But Martha, jogging along in front of me on Tim, turned in the saddle and said, "That's nice of her. You must be getting good. Unlike me."

She finished on a squeak as Tim stumbled ever so slightly but she twisted back to the front and regained her balance.

"Are you having more fun, though?" I asked, squeezing Bramble's sides to extend her walk, so that she came up next to Tim.

"Yeah, it's OK. This morning was pretty good. After Matt finished, we had another look at the foal."

"How's she doing? I meant to go myself but Megan and I got talking."

"She's gorgeous. I tell you, Jess, I'd never want a pony of my own but I wouldn't mind having a foal. No riding, just looking after it, you know. I almost feel like she's mine already cuz we helped her be born."

"I know, I feel the same way. Is Ellie P still talking about buying her?"

Martha shrugged. "I don't know, I don't talk to her and Natalie much; they're pony crazy, like you."

I couldn't help smiling. How cool to be classified with the two girls who were going to have their very own ponies soon.

"Back in line, Jess!" called Mr. Butler.

I eased Bramble into the line behind Tim and watched his beautiful gray shape as he walked steadily along in front of me. Bramble was great to ride, and I loved Bilbo, but Tim would always be "my" pony.

By now we were clear of the cottages and climbing a narrow lane that led onto wide-open hills. We all halted at the top and checked girths and stirrups.

"Time for you two to try cantering," Mr. Butler told Gemma and Martha.

Gemma looked thrilled but Martha immediately said, "No, please not."

"Why not?"

"I don't know how. I might fall off."

"Believe me, it's not difficult and I know you're ready. You might even enjoy it."

Martha looked unconvinced but Mr. Butler was talking to Caroline.

"They can't make me," she whispered to me fiercely.

"Go on, try," I whispered back. "It's the best fun ever. You'll love it."

"I'm not doing it. I'll just trot."

Caroline divided us into three groups. The first included all the bigger ponies – Bramble, Bilbo, Rolo, Star and Blaze. Then came Natalie on Mr. Man, Sarah on Meg and the Ellies on Twinkle and Poppy, and the last group would be the beginners, Gemma and Martha, who'd ride with Mr. Butler.

"We'll lead off," she told me, Mike, Chris and Megan. "We can get a good long canter and we'll halt near those trees right over there in the distance – see? I'll control the pace; no showing off. We don't want any falls."

We nodded and got ready. I shortened the reins just a little and sat slightly forward.

"Don't lean too far, Jess," advised Mr. Butler. "You don't want to give her her head completely."

I nodded and sat more upright, letting the reins slide through my fingers just a little. Caroline kicked Blaze straight into a fast trot and we followed. She waited till we were clear of the other ponies and shouted, "OK, canter!"

All my other canters this week had been very fast but a little uncontrolled. This time I felt really sure of what I was doing. I sat deep into the saddle and pressed Bramble's sides, and felt her change pace from bouncy trot to smooth canter. I kept squeezing rhythmically with my legs to keep her going, keeping my hands as low as I could and letting them go

119

forward and back with her head. She stumbled momentarily, and slowed to a trot, but I shook the reins and gave her a tiny kick, and she moved straight back to canter. The wind rushed past us, my eyes were watering with the cold air, and the soft thud of hoofs filled my ears. It was so cool.

I'd hardly noticed the others. There was so much space that we could spread out and do our own thing. But the trees were rapidly approaching, and Caroline, ahead of us on Blaze, was slowing him and turning him in a big circle. Bramble slowed too, but I didn't want her to do that without my aids. I clicked my tongue and touched her sides to speed her, and waited till we were just beyond all the others before pulling her in. She took immediate notice of me and we trotted around to join the others.

"I thought she was getting away with you there, Jess," said Caroline. "Couldn't you stop?"

"No, there wasn't a problem. I kept her going so I could stop her myself."

"Great. Good control."

More praise! I couldn't believe my luck. Megan grinned at me, perfectly well aware of why I was looking so pleased with myself and generous enough not to mind. She'd ridden well, anyway. Star had a very smooth canter and they always seemed in harmony with each other.

Mike and Chris had raced each other, just keeping the ponies from a full gallop so there wouldn't be trouble, and were arguing over who'd won.

"It was Mike, by a short head!" called Caroline, as she positioned Blaze to make a clear end point.

Chris looked annoyed. "I won," he muttered to me, as if it mattered. I shrugged and turned my attention to the four younger girls. They all knew what they were doing and cantered well, but it didn't look as fast as ours – of course, their ponies were all smaller.

They reached us in a jostling bunch of hot ponies.

Caroline told us to create a line for the beginners, so there'd be no chance of their ponies carrying them away in such open country. I didn't think that was exactly likely; Tim was always obedient and Arthur was such a plodder, Gemma would be lucky to get him to canter at all. But having lost control myself a few times, I could see that it wouldn't do their confidence any good to go into a wild gallop just yet.

We watched as Martha and Gemma walked and then trotted alongside Mr. Butler about halfway toward us.

"Martha doesn't want to canter," I said quietly to Megan.

"Well, it's scary at first. Oh look, they're off!"

Gemma had managed to get Arthur into a slow canter. She was sitting very stiffly, rolling around on the saddle, but even at this distance you could see the enormous grin on her face. And Martha was cantering, too. Mr. Butler had flicked Tim's flank with the very end of his riding crop, and was keeping Captain next to him, controlling his speed and giving Martha encouragement. Martha was holding onto the saddle grimly. She'd managed to keep her feet in the stirrups, which was more than Gemma had by now, but she looked very tense.

They didn't canter for long. Neither girl knew how to balance enough to be able to kick on while cantering, so Tim and Arthur subsided into a trot.

"Well done!" we all yelled, as they came up to us. "Great canter!"

"Not great," said Gemma, her eyes shining, "but it will be next time."

She started telling Megan and Chris exactly what it had been like. I knew just how she was feeling; I could remember how fantastic I'd felt after my first real canter almost a year ago.

Martha more or less fell off as Tim stopped. I jumped off Bramble to get his reins while she got up.

"OK?"

She looked at me and I thought, oh no, she hated it. More pony problems.

"That was …"

She paused and I waited, resigned to hear a negative opinion.

"That was something. That was fantastic. Now I see why you love riding, Jess. Wow!"

Chapter Twelve

You can imagine that shook me a bit.

"That's great," I said tentatively, expecting I'd heard her wrong somehow.

"I never thought I'd be able to go so fast. Just like flying."

"I know."

She left me holding both ponies and ran over to Mr. Butler.

"Can we canter again? Please!"

"We'll see. Maybe later." He glanced over to me and gave the ghost of a wink.

Martha looked dissatisfied but came back over and grabbed Tim's reins.

"I bet we'll canter again tomorrow, especially now that you and Gemma know what to do," I said encouragingly, getting ready to mount Bramble. "And you can work on your trotting this afternoon."

"That's boring, it's only cantering I like. Though maybe jumping might be fun."

Her eyes lit up and I sighed. It was all well and good that she'd finally decided she liked riding, but it sounded as if all she wanted was speed and that wasn't my idea of riding. Of course it was really fun going fast and jumping, but I loved all the careful schooling and just being around ponies in a way that Martha just didn't begin to understand.

Megan brought Star over as we started off again at a gentle trot.

"Well, Gemma's got the riding bug, all right," she commented. "She's been over every single inch of that ride and she's starting all over telling Natalie now."

"But that's good. She was so shy when she came."

"Yes, her confidence has gone way up. What's happened with Martha?"

I explained and Megan laughed. "Poor Jess! You spend all week trying to make her like riding and now that she does it's in the wrong way!"

"Not the wrong way, exactly …"

"I know what you mean. She doesn't really have that special thing about ponies. A fast motorcycle would probably be just as good."

"And wouldn't need grooming every day!"

Mike and Chris joined us and the conversation changed to movies we'd seen and then to music. It was great riding along over beautiful open hills, views stretching in all directions, chatting with good friends. No pressure, no worries. Martha was fine – I checked once or twice – and I wasn't her keeper. Let her enjoy her vacation in her own way.

Mr. Butler led us down off the hills eventually, into a lonely valley. For a long time we rode alongside a river. I kept looking at it and wondering if we'd have to cross it, and if so, how Bramble would respond. Then, suddenly, we veered to the right and, almost without realizing it, we splashed into the shallow water.

Bramble tensed and I kicked her on. For a horrible moment I thought she was going to stop dead … Then Mike and Megan, on either side of me, simultaneously leaned over and gave Bramble an encouraging slap. She reacted by leaping forward; I clung on and kept encouraging her, and in no time at all she'd scrambled out onto dry land.

"Thanks, guys," I said breathlessly, getting control of both my pony and myself. I patted Bramble's neck and told her how clever she was.

"Try again if you'd like," suggested Caroline. "Now that she realizes you're in charge. She was testing the new rider, the other day."

"Do I have to?"

"No. I thought you might like to."

I hesitated. Part of me wanted another try, to prove myself; the other half was worried I'd look like an idiot.

"We'll come across and back with you, OK?" suggested Megan.

Before Bramble or I had time to think about it, the three of us were walking the ponies steadily through the stream and out the other side.

"Let me try alone this time," I said. I encouraged Bramble, and although she went tense under me again, she listened to me whispering, "Go on, you can do it, that's a good girl." She stepped delicately and carefully into the water and then splashed noisily across and out.

"Well done; you shouldn't have any more trouble with her," said Mr. Butler. "Well, since we've stopped, I might as well ask if anyone wants to swap ponies for the last half hour."

I looked around. Maybe it would be good to ride Bilbo again? Everyone quickly opened negotiations.

"Can I try Bramble?" asked Sarah.

"Sure." I passed her the reins and took Meg's. I didn't really want to ride her, but the experience might be interesting.

"Can I try Meg?" asked Martha at my elbow. "Then you could have Tim, just for a while, for old time's sake."

I steadied Meg for Martha and helped her adjust the stirrup leathers while Tim stood patiently waiting for me, his reins looped over my arm. I had to lengthen his stirrups a long way, and once I was up I did feel very close to the ground, but it was great to be on my darling Tim again, the familiar soft

125

leather reins in my hands, his soft, gray mane rippling in front of me. I leaned forward and pulled at his ears the way I knew he loved.

Everyone ended up changing, even Caroline, though the only pony besides Blaze big enough to take her weight was Rolo. Chris was on Bilbo, holding him in tightly and making him walk circles. Natalie had taken Blaze and was shortening stirrups in a very businesslike way. Even Gemma had swapped, with Ellie P, and was looking way too big and heavy for little Poppy; in fact, she looked ridiculous, but no one said anything out loud.

Mike pleaded with Mr. Butler to let him try Captain. I knew what that was about – at Easter, he'd dared Chris to ride Captain, and his competitive instincts must have been galled by knowing that Chris had managed perfectly well.

"He's a big horse," said Mr. Butler, doubtfully (he didn't know anything about the Easter incident), "but if you really want to have a try …"

Mike nodded eagerly and Mr. Butler gave him a leg-up, or he'd never have gotten aboard. He looked like a jockey, perched on top of 17 hand high Captain, and grinned down at me on little Tim from his great height.

Mr. Butler looked around. Most of us had mounted our new ponies – just Ellie T was left, holding Star and her own pony, Twinkle.

"I don't think either of those two could take me," he remarked. "Who's on Blaze? Natalie, you take Twinkle and Ellie can try Star."

"But I'm all ready!" she objected.

"Yes, but I can hardly ride Twinkle. Be reasonable."

Grumbling quietly about beginner's ponies, Natalie slid off Blaze and took Twinkle.

"What difference does it make?" I whispered to Mike.

"She probably wants to prove she can ride him. She and Chris were arguing earlier about who can ride better and riding Twinkle's not exactly going to demonstrate anything."

126

Natalie certainly looked miffed as we started along the track leading back to the farm. I was enjoying Tim; he was so easy to ride, jogging along comfortably, though his mouth wasn't as sensitive to my aids as Bramble. I found myself checking that Sarah was riding Bramble carefully and not pulling at her mouth; in fact, I was so occupied turning around to do that that I forgot to concentrate. Without me guiding him properly, Tim crowded Star in front of us, Star was surprised into a sudden spurt and came up alongside Bilbo, and Bilbo behaved as he always did when he was feeling crowded, by taking a nip at Twinkle.

Understandably, Twinkle shied away, unseating Natalie. She slipped off sideways and landed on the ground with a thump.

She jumped up at once, looking furious.

"Who did that?" she said accusingly. "Chris, if you can't control Bilbo, you shouldn't be riding him!"

"Don't be so stupid!" he shouted back, fighting to control Bilbo who was prancing around excitedly. The rest of us had stopped in a bunch and were keeping well away in case Bilbo felt like taking another bite. "You should keep your pony going when we're in a line; anyone who knows anything about ponies knows that!"

"Uh, it was actually my fault," I put in. "I wasn't watching what Tim was doing. Sorry."

They barely bothered to look at me; they were far too busy yelling at each other. Mr. Butler rode Blaze in between them and told them to be quiet.

"Nobody's hurt; you're just being silly. Natalie, take Twinkle to the head of the line and Chris, take Bilbo to the back and keep him well clear of the others. Jess, for goodness sake pay attention in future."

"Yes, Mr. Butler," we all said. The line started off again and this time I didn't let myself think about anything but riding Tim. By the time we reached the farm, I'd forgotten about the incident and was just enjoying the ride, but as we dismounted it was obvious that Natalie and Chris were still in the middle of their fight.

"What did you think about that?" asked Mike. We had our own ponies back, and he'd tied Bilbo at the end of the fence, next to Bramble and me, to untack and groom.

"What, Chris and Natalie?" I said, ducking under Bramble's belly to undo her girth. "They're just silly. Immature."

"No, me."

I looked up at him. What was I meant to comment about?

"On Captain."

"Oh. Was he OK?"

"Yes. He's hard to ride, though, and he's amazingly strong.

128

Still, I kept him under control. I can feel my arm muscles aching."

"Oh? Good job," I said, absently. I hadn't really noticed, but I realized Mike wanted me to comment. In fact, I think he was disappointed that nobody had actually paid any attention to the way he'd ridden Captain, not even Mr. Butler.

Chris and Natalie kept on sniping at each other all evening. Natalie's friends sided with her and Chris tried to get Megan and me to back him, but we thought the whole argument was a waste of time and said so. That got him even madder. Mike was moody, too. He kept trying to get me to talk with him alone, but I didn't want to. Whenever he did say something to me, it was a cutting comment about somebody else, and it made me feel uncomfortable, talking about people behind their backs. Anyway, Megan and Martha and I had already decided that we'd ask to visit the foal after supper.

"Take a flashlight and don't stay too long," said Mr. Butler. "Be careful not to frighten her."

The yard was pitch dark and reminded us of Tuesday night when Snowdrop gave birth.

"She's all of three days old," said Megan, as we watched the little creature picking her way around her mother.

We tried to keep our voices low and our movements steady. Much braver than before, she came over to see us, and let us stroke her neck. Snowdrop wandered over too and we stroked her and told her how clever she was to have such a gorgeous baby. She lifted her head and whinnied loudly as if she understood, which made us laugh.

Megan went next door to see Campbell. "He looks much better," she reported. "Does anyone know what Matt thought about him?"

"On the mend, he said," said Martha. "He looks like a nice pony. I think I'll choose him if I come again."

Megan and I glanced at each other.

"Coming again?" I remarked, casually.

"Well, you know, maybe," muttered Martha, going pink. "It's not so bad after all."

By the time we got inside, the four girls had gone up to their room. Chris and Mike were playing computer games, and Gemma was reading.

"Anyone want to play a game of cards now that those infants have gone beddy-bye?" said Chris in a loud voice.

"Don't bother, they won't be able to hear you from upstairs," said Megan. "Yeah, why not?"

The tense atmosphere cleared as we played and it turned into a really fun evening. Gemma was displaying an unexpected dry humor and had us all laughing. I thought how much prettier she was now that she was animated. She still had problem hair and skin, but it was what was inside that mattered.

"Time for bed," said Martha, stretching. "Or we'll have Mrs. Butler in here chasing us up."

"She's easier going now that we're a little older," I remarked.

"As she should be. Anyone want to take a stroll outside in the yard before bed?"

Mike looked directly at me as he said that. I went bright red and shook my head.

"I'll come up with you," I said to Martha quickly.

A few minutes later, Megan joined us in the bedroom.

"You want to be careful with Mike," she said to me.

"Don't worry, I can handle him," I said confidently. "I'm hardly going to start wandering around the yard in the middle of the night with him."

"That's not what I meant. I just overheard something he said to Chris, and I'm sure he's out to make trouble with Phil."

"About me?" I said incredulously. "What about me?"

"Trying to make him jealous, I suppose."

"How do you feel about him, Jess?" Martha asked curiously.

I shrugged. "Nothing much. At the beginning of the week I suppose I was flattered that he liked me. He can be so much fun. He says some really funny things."

"Mostly at other people's expense," commented Martha. "I bet he made some really hilarious jokes about me."

I couldn't deny that.

"Well, if I were you I'd forget about him," advised Megan.

"But what about Phil? I like him a lot. I don't want him thinking I've lost interest in him."

"Easy. As soon as we get our phones back, text him and say how much you've missed him being here."

"Yes, and then I'll call him when we get home. That'd be nice."

"Before Mike can get at him."

"Mike won't have his number; they're not friends. Thanks, you two. It's all been a little complicated this week."

"Could've been a lot more if I'd gotten involved with Chris," said Megan.

Martha looked at us both.

"Well, that just does it," she said, in mock seriousness. "I'll have to come back, not for the ponies, but to find a boy who likes me, next time."

Megan caught my eye, and with perfect coordination we launched our pillows straight at Martha.

The next day was our last full one and I jumped out of bed and rushed to the shower the second I woke up, determined not to miss a single moment. Megan heard me and by the time I was ready, she was too. It was still half dark outside. We crept downstairs and out of the house, and jogged over to the paddock. There had been a frost and our breath hung in the air in gray clouds.

"Let's check their water," Megan suggested.

It was frozen, but only lightly, and we broke it easily with the same branch Mike had used. The ponies crowded around us, looking for food. Bramble even nibbled at my coat buttons in case they were good to eat.

"Let's get the hay," I said.

We hefted a couple of bales down to the ponies and stood on the crisp frozen grass, watching them tucking into breakfast. There was a call from the yard and we saw Mr. Butler leaning on the fence.

"Thanks," he said as we hurried up to him. "That's saved me a job. Get the boys to take down a couple more bales after breakfast, will you?"

"Or the girls," said Megan.

"Absolutely right. Whomever you'd like to ask," he said, looking amused.

"What are we doing today?" I asked as we went indoors and started pulling off our boots and gloves.

But all he would say was, "Theory this morning and something exciting this afternoon."

"Too much theory," grumbled Martha when we told her.

"It *is* meant to be a pony management week," Natalie pointed out in a rather superior way.

"Some of us aren't getting our own ponies next month," retaliated Martha.

"Cool down, you two," said Megan. "Haven't we had enough arguments recently?"

"Yes, have you made up with Chris?" I asked.

Natalie tossed her red hair. "That's up to him," she said. "I want an apology for incompetent riding."

"Grow up," said Martha, surprisingly. "All that happened was that you fell off. We all do that."

There wasn't time for more. Mr. Butler came in and told us we'd be doing tack cleaning and then some theory, followed by the mysterious "fun" in the afternoon.

132

"What do you think it will be?" asked Gemma as we settled ourselves in the tack room with metal polish and old rags.

"Some sort of ride, I'm sure," I said. "We had a terrific treasure hunt the first time I was here."

"Which we won," said Mike, plunking himself down next to me. "And which Chris lost."

Chris grinned from the other side of the room. He seemed to have completely forgotten the fight with Natalie and was being cheerful and friendly.

"We did gymkhana games my first time," remembered Sarah.

All of us who'd been to the center before had done that. We compared our experiences and concluded that the dress-up race had usually been the most fun.

"Though I like the bending best," said Natalie, predictably. "It tests your riding better."

There was a general groan. Everyone else seemed to feel that Natalie was a pain, too.

"When you have your own pony, you can bend it as much as you like," said Mike, "Just be careful it doesn't snap."

"Ellie, what sort of pony do you want?" I asked, trying to find a safer subject.

The conversation settled down. After a while, we went indoors for the theory. On the way, Ellie P said to me, "Try and keep Chris off Nat for us, if you can. It'd be nice not to have her moaning at us all the time."

"I'll do my best," I promised. "Why's she gotten so touchy?"

"It's just the way she is. She likes to be best and so does Chris."

"OK. I'll see what I can do."

"And Jess – when I get my pony, I'll call you and maybe you'd like to come and stay and try him?"

"That would be great," I promised. "Really great."

Chapter Thirteen

The theory session turned out to be tailor-made for Natalie and Ellie because it was all about buying a pony. We were divided into groups of two and had to identify pony breeds.

The next discussion was about telling a pony's age. We looked at some illustrations of teeth and Mr. Butler explained how you could tell by the way the teeth change. It all looked very complicated and unlikely to me.

"We'll try it out this afternoon," he suggested. "You can all have a try guessing Captain's age, as I know that exactly. There'll be a prize for the person who gets it right."

Then, in groups of two, we had to come up with some things to consider if we were buying a pony. After we had all created lengthy lists, Mr. Butler finally said, "OK, you seem to have run out of ideas. I think that's enough theory for one day. Early lunch and then out in the yard with your ponies tacked up and ready by one thirty. Go, go, go!"

Over lunch, Megan and I talked about the ponies we'd buy until Martha broke in and said we were getting boring and would we please talk about something else, anything else. But even she had to get back to ponies soon as almost immediately after that it was time to catch the ponies.

"The last ride," I said mournfully, as I led Bramble into

the yard and tied her to the fence. "I can't believe the week's almost over."

"At least we *are* riding," said Megan, practically, fastening Star's girth. "It could've been pouring rain all day."

We were soon ready. Even Gemma and Martha could tack up fast now, after a week's practice.

"Before we start, have a look in your pony's mouth and see how old you think he is," Mr. Butler said.

"Do we have to?" Martha muttered to me. "I mean, I know Tim's a sweetie, but he's got monster teeth."

"All the better to eat you with? Let me."

I lifted Tim's lips gently and we peered at his teeth.

"What are we looking for?" I asked.

Martha pulled out a piece of paper with the illustrations. "Count backwards from the front. How many teeth?"

"Three big ones this side."

"So he's four or more."

"Well, obviously, he's been here for at least three years."

"Is there a little tooth further back?"

I lifted another flap of lip and there it was "Anything else?"

"See if there's a sort of hook inside the third tooth back at the top."

I wasn't so sure I wanted to put my hand right inside Tim's mouth, but I wasn't going to show Martha I was bothered. And after all, I'd slipped a metal bit into his mouth numerous times. It was warm and I could feel his tongue against my hand. Weird.

"Maybe there's something," I said. "What does that mean?"

"He should be six or seven."

"That sounds right. Shall we try Bramble?"

Bramble's teeth sloped more than Tim's, and when we looked carefully there was a tiny groove in the third tooth, which made her a bit older, maybe ten. I couldn't find the little extra tooth, though.

"How are you doing?" asked Mr. Butler.

We told him what we'd found and he nodded. "That's about right. Bramble's a mare and for some reason tushes – those are the extra teeth – don't grow in mares. She's certainly three or four years older than Tim. OK, everyone," he raised his voice, "have a look at Captain."

We crowded around and all looked earnestly inside, as if we were medical students or something. I'd never noticed before how many massive back teeth horses and ponies have. There's a neat gap between the back teeth and the front ones where the metal bit goes.

"There's a tush thingy," said Martha, looking at the extra teeth.

"And I think there's a teeny weeny groove on that tooth," said Natalie.

"So that makes him …?"

"About ten," said Chris, triumphantly, after checking his diagram. "Am I right or am I right?"

"Dead on. He turned ten this spring. And your prize is …" Mr. Butler gave him a bar of chocolate. "OK, you may want to wash hands after that and then I'll tell you what we're doing."

"Jumping?" asked Megan hopefully.

"Probably, but don't worry, Gemma and Martha, you don't have to."

"Gymkhana games?" suggested Megan.

"Sorry, no. It's not warm enough to be standing around waiting for your turn, and it wouldn't do the paddock much good for all the grass to be churned up. No, you're going to do a paper chase."

"What's that?"

"You may have noticed Caroline's not around?"

We all nodded.

"She's been out laying a trail, and our job – your job, I should say, as you're going to do all the work, is to follow it."

"Great," said Chris. "Are there prizes?"

"Let me make one thing perfectly clear. This isn't a race, or even a competition. You've got to work together, as a team, to find the next clue, and it won't always be easy. Caroline's had strict instructions from me not to leave the trail too close together."

"And the bits might blow away," someone said.

"Hopefully not. The forecast's for a dry, still afternoon, just right for a good ride. Now, we agreed to start in the field down the lane, so I'd like to see a good steady walk along the lane, all in single file this time, please, Jess, and we'll gather inside the field and start looking."

"Not that there's much choice in that field," Mike said to no one in particular as we left the yard, "as we always take that same track. Hey, watch out! Yuk!"

Bramble had lifted her tail and deposited a steaming pile of manure right in front of Bilbo, who understandably sidestepped and nearly tipped Mike off.

"Sorry," I said, "I didn't know you were so close behind."

He glowered at me. "Can't you control that animal?"

"Yes I can!' I answered, nettled. "But I can't actually house train her any more than you could."

"Yeah, well, you could be more careful," he grumbled, though I didn't see how. He kicked Bilbo into a trot to overtake me.

"I said walk," yelled Mr. Butler, "so walk!"

Mike pulled Bilbo in front of me and sat slouched in the saddle, ignoring the happy chatter that flew up and down the line. As soon as we got into the field and could spread out, I took Bramble up to him and asked if there was something wrong.

"What d'you think?" he grouched.

"How should I know? That's why I'm asking you."

"Well, don't waste your breath."

He steered Bilbo away from me.

Megan came over. "What's gotten into him?"

"I wish I knew; he can't think I *made* Bramble do a poop, and anyway it didn't land *on* Bilbo."

"It was a very near miss, though," she said, giggling. "Kerplunk! Splat!"

That made me giggle too. I told her about the first vacation, when I'd been too close to Twinkle and only just escaped being splatted myself. Martha and Gemma joined us and Gemma said, "The thing that threw me was when Arthur did a pee the first time. There I was sitting kicking like mad, and he didn't move an inch. You feel like such a fool."

"It happens to all of us," I said. "So, has anyone seen the first slip of paper?"

There was a shout from where the track left the field, where, inevitably, Caroline must have gone. We all gathered there and Mr. Butler said he'd bring up the rear.

"Because we don't want any stragglers getting lost this time," he said, looking at Chris and me. "Remember, if you're at the front, make sure everyone knows where to go."

"Do you know the route?" asked Sarah.

"No. I told Caroline not to tell me," he said, though I'm not sure I believed him.

We walked steadily down the long hill where I'd cantered dramatically with Megan and reached the fork. It took a while to find a paper clue; Caroline had tucked it in a tree trunk around the corner to the left. That took us along by the tree trunks.

"Can we jump?" I asked.

"Same as before, but take care – we don't want anyone coming off. The ground's extra muddy and you'd get soaked."

So we took turns jumping the short course, and just as she was before Bramble was great, lifting easily over the obstacles and landing sweetly. I really didn't have to do anything except lean a bit forward. Gemma and Martha walked their ponies sedately alongside with Mr. Butler as the rest of us whizzed by and went back for second jumps.

"Can't we try?" Gemma pleaded.

"Not yet. There'll be some lower jumps later – at least, I guess there will," he corrected himself swiftly.

So he does know where we're going, I thought. No one else seemed to notice, and anyway it didn't take away the fun of searching for each piece of paper. Caroline had been careful not to leave many and it sometimes took a long time to figure out which way to go. Her route led us up onto the hills and there it was even harder to locate clues. She'd usually anchored them under stones or stuffed them into clumps of heather where they were hidden unless you were really near. We all got really involved in looking, riding with our eyes to the ground, raking it for glimpses of white.

"This way!" yelled Chris. He was way in the distance

almost out of sight over a hill. I could just see him waving if I stood in the stirrups.

"Coming!" I shouted back. Bramble took off satisfactorily into a swift canter up and over the hillock. Star thundered along parallel to us, and not far off Sarah on Meg was doing the same. I could feel Bramble realizing she was in a race … We flew over the soft grass, holding on tight as the ponies swerved around tussocks and rabbit holes, shouting for joy.

"Whoa!" Megan sang out as we got closer to Chris. We quickly slowed the ponies and managed to arrive in good shape, and Mr. Butler didn't seem to mind that we'd been racing.

"It looks like we have to go into the woods over there," Natalie said, cantering toward us from further down the hill. "I just found a sheet of paper half way there."

"Be careful on the slope, everyone; it's slippery," Mr. Butler warned as we entered the woods. There wasn't a path; we had to ride between the trees, ducking and leaning sideways to avoid being hit by stray branches.

"I've worked out what the problem is," I said to Ellie P.

"What problem?"

"Why we keep nearly getting knocked off. The ponies go through where they know they have room; they just don't allow for us on top of them."

"Well, I wish they'd learn," said Ellie, as a stray branch nearly tipped her hat off.

"The trick is for you to do the work," said Natalie. "It's no good just sitting on the pony and letting him choose his own path. You have to steer."

"Hurry up, you guys!" called Megan. "There's an evil hill coming up!"

We gathered at the top of the steep bank. It was thick with dead leaves and broken up by undergrowth and trees.

"How do we get down there? There's no path," Martha asked nervously.

"You've got a choice," said Mr. Butler, reining Captain well in. "Either you can get off and lead your pony; that's a good idea if you feel at all worried at the thought of riding down. Or if you're feeling brave, follow the line I take but hang on tight – and watch for low branches."

Martha slid off instantly, and so did Ellie T, who wasn't a very confident rider. They held their ponies' bridles firmly near the pony's mouths and started to edge downwards, taking a wide diagonal line across the hillside. It wasn't sheer or anything like that, but I could understand why they were nervous about riding down it. I didn't like the idea of letting Bramble slip, either.

The rest of the group bunched up and followed Captain. Mr. Butler went to one side for a while, and then doubled back in a kind of zigzag, back and forth, crossing Ellie and Martha who were progressing slowly and carefully. What we were doing resembled skiing, and the hard part was turning the other way, because for a moment we had to face straight downhill. Also, gravity was trying to make us fall to the downhill side of the pony, and my saddle seemed especially slippery that afternoon. Too much saddle soap when we were cleaning tack, I told myself, catching hold of the pommel to keep from falling sideways. That'll teach me to be enthusiastic about doing it properly.

Mr. Butler looked back up at the zigzagging line.

"Concentrate on keeping your weight centralized, and grip with your knees and thighs," he advised. "Don't worry about sliding. And don't forget, lean forward."

I tried focusing as he said, and he was right, it was easier. It seemed natural to lean backwards to help my pony, but actually it was the worst thing to do, as it unbalanced her and made it difficult for her to keep a grip on the slippery ground. I also had to fight an instinct to hold her in very tightly; she needed to have enough rein to stretch her neck, even though that made me feel less safe.

"Relax a bit, Jess," called Mr. Butler. "You're tensing up and that doesn't help Bramble."

"Easier said than done," I puffed to Megan, who was looking cool and competent as Star carefully picked her way downhill. "I don't think Bramble's enjoying this any more than I am."

"Don't worry, we're nearly at the bottom," she said.

I hadn't realized how far we'd come. The slope widened and steepened further into a little hollow and then there was a sharp slope up and out the other side and what looked like flat ground beyond.

"Go on, Bramble," I urged, as she hesitated and nearly stopped. "Not far now."

I gave her an encouraging kick, but unfortunately she misinterpreted it. She changed from walk to a rapid trot just as we reached the steepest point so far, entering the little hollow, and carried me swiftly past the ponies ahead, making them swerve and unsettling their riders, and sweeping past Mr. Butler. Carried away by her own momentum, like when you run down a steep hill and can't stop yourself, she broke into a ragged canter that completely made me lose balance and control. Struggling to gather the reins, my feet half out of the stirrups, I couldn't stop her accelerating up the hill opposite. I was much too far back in the saddle, bouncing all over the place. It was like a losing battle with gravity. Bramble went up and up, I slid back and back, and the inevitable moment arrived when our connection finally failed, and I fell, backwards, over her hind side, and landed with a thump and a roll onto the ground. For a few muddled seconds I rolled back downhill, confused and disoriented. Then I was down in the base of the hollow, curled up in a muddy ball, and all around me were the other ponies with their sharp, heavy hoofs.

Chapter Fourteen

A stab of instinctive panic shot through me as I looked at the web of horse legs, and then up at their bulky bodies. It resolved almost immediately into relief that I wasn't hurt at all from the fall and that the ponies weren't going to step on me, not only because they wouldn't want to but also because their riders were skillfully veering them away from my body. Voices slowly penetrated the eerie silence that had been all I could hear at first.

"Jess?"

"Are you all right?"

"Say something!"

"She's unconscious!"

"No, no, I'm not!" I managed to say, hauling myself back onto slightly unsteady legs. "I'm OK."

Mr. Butler had jumped down and stood facing me, with Captain absurdly looking at me too over his shoulder.

"Did you hit your head?" he said, urgently.

"No," I replied. I knew how important it was that he knew I didn't have a concussion; I'd been the embarrassing cause for a delay once before, at the start of the trail riding vacation.

"Absolutely sure?"

"Absolutely."

"Check her out by asking her questions," suggested

Mike with a malevolent grin. "Name? Rank? Serial number?"

"I'm not in the army," I answered weakly. "And I *didn't* hit my head."

"What about the rest of you? Do you hurt anywhere?"

I flexed my arms and legs. Nothing gave any pain apart from a general ache, which I knew would show itself in some great bruises in a day or two.

"I'm fine."

"It looked mega dramatic, your falling back down the hill like that," said Sarah.

"And landing slap bang at our feet," added Chris.

"Yeah, well, that was the part I didn't enjoy," I admitted, managing to laugh at the memory. "Trusting you all to control your ponies …"

Megan pushed through the crowd on foot, leading Star and Bramble.

"Poor old Bramble, she didn't like that much either," I said, stroking her nose. She tossed her head away but I held onto her noseband and stroked some more and soon she calmed down and was pushing her head into my armpit in her usual friendly way.

"Give her a piece of carrot," said Mr. Butler, who usually had a few in his pocket. "Just to make her feel good again."

I held the carrot on my flat palm, as you always do, and felt Bramble's soft lips nuzzling for it. For a second, you can feel the teeth against your skin, but as long as your hand's flat, you don't get bitten. Bramble crunched happily, dribbling orange down the sides of her mouth. You're not normally meant to feed ponies when they're bridled as the bit gets in the way and gets all messy, but special treats are different.

"Ready to mount?"

I nodded and went around to Bramble's side. Her saddle had slipped a little as I fell, so I had to pull it forward and adjust the girth. Then I got my foot into the stirrup as my

144

hands, holding the reins, pushed down on her back, and swung up into the saddle. I felt with my right foot for the other stirrup, gathered the reins till I felt I'd connected with Bramble's mouth, and was ready to start again.

"I've found the next paper," said Ellie P. "It's over there."

We set off through light woodland. Bramble and I jogged along contentedly, generally getting our breaths back after the drama. All around us the others were talking and laughing and joking. Despite a few sore patches, I thought how lucky I was to be there, and how much I didn't want the week to end. I was looking forward to seeing my family again, of course – and I suddenly remembered that they were coming to pick us up tomorrow morning, and I'd be able to show the ponies to the twins. They'd come last summer too, but when you're only a year old you don't register much, and now they were almost two. I wondered if I would be able to sit them on a pony, just to get the feel of it, and wouldn't Mom just love the foal! Dad might too, of course, but somehow I thought it was more a girly thing to like baby animals. I'd be able to show Dad how much better I was around horses now, too, even though they wouldn't see me ride. Maybe I should take up their offer of riding lessons, or try to earn money for them myself. Maybe I was wimping out by not taking them. I resolved to have a good long talk with Mom and Dad about my future as soon as I could, and enlist them into my dream of becoming a seriously good rider …

"Jess!"

"What?"

"Watch out!"

About six people were yelling at me; I hadn't even noticed that we were out of the woods and riding along the edge of a ploughed field, nor that Bramble had wandered vaguely off the grassy edge and was slogging fetlock-deep in gooey mud.

I guided her back onto the grass. There was a gross oozing

noise as she pulled her feet out of the ground and there'd be some tough grooming ahead.

Mr. Butler had halted and waved the other riders past as he waited for me.

"Are you really and truly sure you're OK?" he asked. "You don't have a headache or anything?"

I went bright red. "Really and truly. I just wasn't concentrating."

"Well, in that case, pull yourself together. It's the last afternoon – don't spoil it for everyone."

He trotted on ahead. Megan joined me.

"That was unfair," she said. "It wasn't your fault you fell off."

"No, but it was my fault that I let Bramble leave the shoulder," I admitted. "I shouldn't have done that."

"Never mind," Megan said comfortingly, "Let's enjoy ourselves. Have you seen Martha? She's doing really well."

We'd shifted into a trot and I could see Martha three ponies ahead, rising and falling in perfect rhythm. She was sitting well with a straight back and she was even managing to keep her hands low.

"If you'd asked me on Wednesday, I'd have sworn she'd never take to riding," Megan said.

"I still don't think she likes it like we do."

Megan laughed. "That applies to most people. Even I don't like it like you do, and I love it."

I started telling her what I'd been thinking, about riding lessons, and she was really encouraging and made me realize how unnecessarily silly I'd been before. But all this time I made sure I was focusing on riding properly, too, and not likely to attract any more attention from Mr. Butler.

Caroline's route took us through several fields. The first couple had open gates, but the barrier between the next two was an open ditch, about a yard wide, with a narrow plank bridge across it. Mr. Butler waited till we were all gathered.

"I don't love the idea of riding over that," said Gemma, looking worried. "What happens if he puts a foot over the edge?"

"You get wet," said Mike sardonically. "Obviously."

"Can't we jump the ditch?" asked Natalie.

"Well, that's one option," said Mr. Butler, frowning at Mike. "Or if you prefer you can dismount and lead your pony over the bridge."

We peered into the ditch. It was deep and murky.

Martha slid off Tim. "I'm walking," she said firmly. "No way am I jumping that."

Ellie T and Gemma joined her. Walking gingerly, they took turns leading their ponies across the bridge. It wobbled alarmingly under their weight but the ponies plodded across without making a fuss.

"Are the rest of you going to jump?" asked Mr. Butler.

We all nodded, though a little bubble of fear was curling up my stomach.

"Mike first, then Natalie," he said. "The rest of you, watch how they do it."

Mike took Bilbo back a few yards, approached at a canter, kicked at just the right moment, and let Bilbo soar over the ditch. Natalie followed more slowly, but efficiently.

"That is *so* easy," Mike said from the other side.

"Megan and Jess next," said Mr. Butler. "Jess, just follow Megan and you'll be fine."

We positioned the ponies and I let Bramble follow Star into a steady trot. Don't think about not getting over, I told myself. Just think of it like a log. But it was hard not to think of that cold, deep water waiting to make me look stupid if I fell in.

Megan pressed Star's sides and a short distance behind, I copied. We cantered, and Star lifted into a jump. I concentrated on keeping the canter going and then leaning forward just before the ditch. For one awful moment I thought Bramble was going to refuse and I'd fall forward over her

head into the water – but she didn't. She jumped and landed on the other side and we were over.

"Nice one," said Megan. We grinned at each other and at Natalie. Mike wasn't looking at us. Muttering under his breath, he was watching Chris as Rolo pounded toward the ditch, and I'd swear he was disappointed when Chris made it over, followed by Sarah, panting and red-faced but OK.

That just left Ellie P. and Mr. Butler. Poppy wasn't big but I knew she could jump well. Ellie thumped her sides energetically to get her cantering hard, flew toward the ditch, flapping her elbows as she went in her enthusiasm to keep her going, and kicked her into a jump. Poppy took off, but even to my fairly inexperienced eye, it looked a little too soon. She was stretched out over the water, but her front legs were coming down and she'd barely cleared the far edge, and her back legs …

There was a breathless moment of slow motion as we waited to see if Poppy would make it. Ellie leaned forward so far she was practically parallel with Poppy's nose. She was glancing down and obviously only too aware of how easily she might land in the ditch instead of safely on dry land. Then Poppy's front legs were on the grass, and her back legs tucked under her and just, just gripped the very edge of the ditch. She even started to slide back in, but Ellie's weight was so far forward and the impetus of the jump was so strong that Poppy scrambled up and over, and she was clear, greeted by the sound of our cheers.

Mr. Butler popped over the ditch on Captain as if it was nothing at all.

"You all certainly like action," he commented. "We've had a lot of it this afternoon."

"Except that Martha and I still haven't jumped," mentioned Gemma, eagerly. "And you did promise ..."

Mr. Butler looked around at all of us. "Everyone happy to do just a little more? Easy stuff," he added.

We all said yes, of course, though I don't think some of us minded the thought of an easier jump.

"Aren't we following the paper any more?" asked Martha. We'd almost forgotten about that.

"I know where we are, anyway," said Natalie. "It's not far to the farm, is it?'"

"True, but it won't hurt to look for the trail, just in case Caroline's put in a detour,' suggested Mr. Butler.

Sarah picked up the trail along a wide track that I recognized, too. We cantered for a while, with Mr. Butler at the back with the two novices, keeping an eye on them. Then Chris, eagle-eyed as always, spotted a piece of paper down a narrow side path, so we walked the ponies along that, and shortly came to a line of narrow branches across the path, none of them more than six inches high.

"It can't be a coincidence," I whispered to Martha. "He knew we'd get here."

"How do I jump them?" she said, sounding panicky.

"You don't, really," I said. "Tim will hardly leave the ground. Just trot and he'll do it for you."

"And lean forward just a little," advised Megan.

Mr. Butler told us to keep going at a trot, and the ponies followed each other along the little course. It was easy if you knew what you were doing, but Gemma and Martha were both practically bursting with pride when they'd completed it and begged for another try and then another.

"Enough's enough," said Mr. Butler at last. "It's time to be getting back."

The slow procession of ponies and riders wound uphill in the last stretch of woodland, and clattered along the lane in a leisurely end-of-day rhythm that filled me with happiness and sadness at the same time. Martha was still glowing with excitement as we untacked the ponies and groomed them for the last time this vacation. I turned Bramble out into the paddock and watched her kick up her heels and canter down to join her friends, and wondered when I'd be back next, and which pony I'd ride, and what adventures we'd have.

But first, we had a final evening and a chance to show my family around tomorrow, so I didn't need to say goodbye to Bramble and Bilbo and Tim just yet. After showers and clean clothes – and did I need clean clothes after my fall – we crammed into the common room to hear that we'd be having a party. Mrs. Butler had cooked all sorts of delicious food, which was laid out on the table in the next room, and Caroline had set up disco lights and was playing funky music.

"Great trail," we told her.

"Especially the ditch," I added.

We told her all about the afternoon. She'd had fun setting up the trail and was really pleased it had been so successful.

"I spent the afternoon with Snowdrop and her foal," she

150

told us. "They're doing so well that now that it's warmer we'll put them in the paddock."

"Will they be safe with the other ponies?" Sarah asked.

"We might keep them separate for a day or two. They'll have other company soon – the farmer next door's putting a flock of sheep in the next field and they'll be lambing soon."

"How nice," I sighed. "If only we could be here to see them."

Caroline looked at me a little oddly. "Maybe you will," she said.

Everyone started dancing then, and I didn't think any more about her comment. We had a great evening, playing silly games, dancing, joking and laughing. Mike had stopped sulking, but he and I kept apart. I think he'd realized he wasn't going to get anywhere with me. I was already planning the text message that I'd send Phil, telling him about my week, the minute I got my cell phone back.

Megan nudged me in amusement late in the evening. "Just look at those two," she murmured. Chris and Natalie, as she'd predicted, were deep in conversation, and they were holding hands. "A matched pair," she added, dryly.

So that was the end of my third vacation at the farm; except for the one amazing thing that happened the next day, after Mom and Dad and the twins rolled up in the car, waving wildly. We hugged and kissed each other, and then Dad took me over to the paddock fence and leaned on it with me.

"I have some news, Jess," he said, "important news."

I looked at him in alarm. "Is everyone all right?"

"Everyone's fine. In fact, I think soon everyone's going to be more than fine. We didn't want to tell you until the end of this week, till everything was settled, but now it is."

"What is?' I said impatiently. "Dad, what's going on?"

He looked around at the beautiful scene: clear sky, clean green grass, ponies grazing, Snowdrop and her foal standing bemusedly in a fenced off area, and everything I loved so much.

"You know I said I was getting a promotion," he said.

"Yes?"

"How would you feel if I said it would involve moving?"

"Moving? What, leaving our house?"

"And your school."

"I don't know," I said hesitantly. "Leaving all my friends ... we've always lived there."

"True."

I looked at Dad suspiciously. His eyes were twinkling in the way they only do when something truly, spectacularly happy is happening.

"Dad, where are we going?"

He put an arm around my shoulders and squeezed them. "Well, Jess, you might not believe me, but I had a choice, and we've chosen. It's here."

"Here?"

I couldn't believe my ears. "Here, at the farm? What about the Butlers?"

"Not here at the farm, but here in the country. We're going to move to this area, probably to the village down the road, and you'll be able to come here to ride. Now, what do you think of that?"

I don't think I've got the words to describe how I felt, so I'll leave you to imagine it. Living in the country, living near the farm, riding all the time! I turned around slowly and looked at everything, the place, the ponies, my friends, and I found something to say.

"Oh Dad," I said, "that will be just perfect."